MARGARET MORGAN
and
MARY MORGAN PEDLOW
Memorial
RIVERSIDE PUBLIC LIBRARY

Wildfire

Wildfire

Cathie Linz

G.K. Hall & Co. • Chivers Press
Thorndike, Maine USA Bath, Avon, England

This Large Print edition is published by G.K. Hall & Co., USA and by Chivers Press, England.

Published in 1996 in the U.S. by arrangement with Cathie L. Baumgardner.

Published in 1996 in the U.K. by arrangement with the author.

U.S. Hardcover 0-7838-1652-9 (Romance Collection Edition)
U.K. Hardcover 0-7451-4770-4 (Chivers Large Print)

G.K. Hall Large Print Romance Collection.

The text of this Large Print edition is unabridged.
Other aspects of the book may vary from the original edition.

Set in 16 pt. News Plantin by Minnie B. Raven.

Printed in the United States on permanent paper.

British Library Cataloguing in Publication Data available

Library of Congress Cataloging in Publication Data

Linz, Cathie.
Wildfire / Cathie Linz.
p. cm.
ISBN 0-7838-1652-9 (lg. print: hc)
1. Large type books. I. Title.
[PS3562.I558W55 1996]
813'.54—dc20 95-53789

Wildfire

Chapter One

The glass-encased fire alarm had ended a sedate existence, embedded as it was in the wall of Deerfield College's library. Indeed, its only moments of excitement were the periodic checks by the Wisconsin State safety inspector. But today its moment had come. A feminine hand, betraying only the slightest tremor, reached out and successfully activated the alarm system.

"This is not a drill!" Amanda Richards pivoted to briskly inform the students occupying the library study cubicles. "Don't panic, you're not in any immediate danger. Please leave the building, using the fire doors at the ends of the stacks." Her instructions were clearly audible even over the sudden babble of raised voices, and her inflection held an authority that the students responded to without question.

As associate librarian, Amanda was very much aware of her responsibilities. Never one to panic in a crisis, she supervised the evacuation, checking to make certain that everyone was out before leaving herself. The other department heads would make sure that their individual sections of the library were also evacuated, thanks to the revised emergency disaster plan that Amanda had initiated only last week.

Located amid rolling hillsides in southern Wisconsin, Deerfield College had the reputation of being an excellent private liberal arts college. Its mellow brick buildings, clustered around a small lake like a group of campers around a campfire, blended well with their natural surroundings. But today that sense of harmony was shattered by the high-pitched wail of a siren heralding the arrival of Deerfield's fire department.

Amanda arrived at the front entrance in time to see the firemen scramble off the multi-laddered truck and enter the building. She prayed that the fire could be contained before it reached the library proper and did irreversible damage. As it was, the flames had no doubt ruined the contents of the library's storage room, where she'd discovered the blaze.

Amanda adeptly side-stepped a group of students who were busy speculating about the fire and its possible cause. Before catching sight of her coworkers, she overheard one disgruntled student actually suggest that it was all a freshman prank.

Hurrying over to join them, she directed her first question to the circulation librarian. "Did you make sure your section was cleared?"

"We got all the students out," Connie Stillman confirmed. "They weren't very pleased about it though. They didn't believe that there was really a fire. Who set off the alarm?"

"I did," Amanda replied. "The fire was down in the storage room."

A breathless voice interrupted the rest of her

explanation. "Amanda! Thank heavens you're all right!"

Helen Liggett was one of the two assistants in Technical Services. Since Amanda had held the position of head of that department before becoming associate librarian, she knew Helen quite well. In her early sixties, Helen had a natural exuberance that defied her chronological age, but she'd always brooded over Amanda like an adoptive mother hen.

At the other end of the spectrum was Susan, the second assistant, who at twenty was looking for a husband in this year's crop of college seniors. While Helen fretted over the possible damage, Susan viewed the day's occurrence as a spot of excitement in an otherwise dull day.

"Boy, is Beth going to be sorry that she missed this!" Susan exclaimed. "What a lousy time to be out sick!"

Beth Kent had recently been promoted from cataloging librarian to head of Technical Services. Closer to Amanda's own age, twenty-five to her thirty, the two had become good friends.

The arrival of John Abbington, the head librarian, precluded further speculation about Beth's reaction to missing the fire.

"Well, girls," he boomed with false joviality. "I see you all made it out without mishap."

Amanda gritted her teeth at his use of the term *girls.* The title didn't apply to any of the women standing before him. Stifling her immense irritation, she quickly asked, "Have you gotten a damage report yet?"

"No, I haven't, but the dean's just informed me that the entire building will be closed for the remainder of the day. Once the embers have been doused and the fire department deems it safe, you may all return for your personal belongings and then go home," he instructed with a paternalistic smile.

Home for Amanda was the white frame house she'd grown up in. Her father had once been a professor at Deerfield College, before taking a job at a prestigious ivy-league university in New England. Amanda had never settled in after the move, perhaps because she sensed the growing discontentment between her parents, who went through a bitter divorce a few years later. At fifteen Amanda had been shuttled back and forth between her father in New England and her mother's new home in California. It was little wonder that she learned to be self-sufficient at an early age and to distrust the institution of marriage.

Now she was back in Deerfield, had been for the past six years. In that time she'd been professionally successful, quickly rising to her present position of second in command in the library's hierarchy. She'd also managed, with careful planning, to buy the very house she'd grown up in when it had gone on the market.

Back at work the next morning Amanda spent fifteen minutes fruitlessly searching for the papers she needed to complete a summary of the fire damage before remembering that she'd had the list in her hand right before discovering the blaze. With an impatient sigh at the time already wasted she left her office and headed for the stairway leading to the basement. While slowly descending the steps she scanned their surface for the multi-paged document. A rope strung across the bottom of the stairway cordoned off the affected area and halted her progress. Only one overhead light was lit and it did little to alleviate the shadowy interior of the basement. She might not have noticed the man bent over the pile of charred rubble in the corner if he hadn't shifted suddenly, dislodging something.

Amanda immediately backed away, her mouth dry with fear. If this was the man who had started the fire, there was no telling what he'd do if he discovered her there. Should she call the police? No, they'd take too long to get there; the man could well be gone by then. It would undoubtedly be faster to call college security.

She punched out their extension on the nearest phone and moments later a security guard dutifully arrived. Amanda followed him downstairs, feeling very much like a character in one of the mysteries she loved to read.

The intruder was standing now, but his back was still turned to them. His dark curly head was bent while he wrote something in a small notebook that suddenly fell to the tanned leather of his boots as the guard grabbed him from behind.

"Listen, buddy, this is a restricted area!" the guard growled. "Can't you read? Or were you coming back to start another little fire? I want to see some form of ID and I want to see it now!"

"Fine." The trespasser's voice was unruffled. "If you'd stop the Kojak impersonation and let me go, I'd be more than happy to show it to you."

"I'm not letting you go until I see that ID. Ms. Richards, would you get his wallet, please?"

Shackled by the guard's viselike hold on his arms, the stranger shrugged and agreed with sardonic humor. "You do that, Ms. Richards. I've always wanted to be frisked by a librarian."

Determined not to be affected by the intruder's suggestive remark, Amanda donned her professional mantle. "Do you keep your wallet in your left or right pocket?" Her voice bristled with crispness.

"Left," was the laconic reply.

While not a prude, Amanda was not accustomed to reaching her hands into strange men's pockets. The denim of his jeans may have been soft from numerous washings, but the body beneath was powerfully firm. The jeans were so tightly molded to his muscular form that she could barely squeeze her fingers into the pocket, and then they were trapped between the two layers of denim. With a naughty look that suggested it had been her idea to investigate his jeans, the stranger added one important note to his directions. "In my vest."

Amanda snatched her hand back, as though it had been burned, and indeed it felt remarkably singed. The news that his wallet was in his vest shouldn't have surprised her. He couldn't keep it in his pants pocket like most men did; the jeans were too tight for anything to fit in those pockets, including her fingers!

Cool it, she firmly instructed her increased heartbeat. Her own intense awareness of him threw her, but no more so than the cold metal she discovered when she inadvertently fumbled under the right rather than the left side of his vest.

"He's carrying a gun!" she gasped, retreating to a safe distance.

Angered by her evident fear, the stranger suddenly lost patience. "Of course I'm carrying a gun," he snapped. "I'm a cop!"

The security guard made no comment; he merely tightened his grip and nodded to Amanda to continue. On her second attempt she located the wallet with no difficulty, although her fingers shook as she flipped it open. There, staring up at her, was the face of the man before her, and beneath the photograph were both his name and position. Brady Gallagher, Detective. Across from it was his police badge.

Eyeing the substantiating evidence, the college security guard quickly released him, embarrassment reddening his face as he apologized for the mistake.

"Never mind," Brady dismissed. "I know you

were only doing your job."

Relieved to be let off the hook, the guard quickly took his leave. Amanda, however, was not allowed the same privilege. "Just a moment, Ms. Richards. I'd like a word with you."

"Yes?"

"I hope you don't have the same trouble identifying right from wrong as you do right from left." His tone was one of mocking amusement. "If you had followed directions, you wouldn't have been shocked."

"I find your manner insulting, Detective Gallagher," she haughtily informed him.

"Call me Brady," he instructed, unimpressed by her frigid tone. "It'll be easier."

For whom? she wondered uneasily, not liking the way his dark eyes were assessing her, taking stock of her from head to toe and resting on every curve in between with more than casual interest.

"As for being insulting, my most humble apologies. Put it down to the disturbing experience of being frisked by you. For future reference, Ms. Richards, I carry my gun on my right side and my wallet on my left."

"Thank you for that extremely useless piece of information, Detective Gallagher."

"Think nothing of it."

"I'll do that," Amanda obligingly agreed.

The infuriating man had the nerve to grin!

"Do you think we could continue this discussion upstairs?" Amanda requested in what she was pleased to note were even tones that reflected none of her inner agitation.

"Certainly." She caught a flash of silver binding his wrist as he motioned her ahead. "After you."

As Amanda mounted the stairs she was very much aware of Brady Gallagher's presence behind her. The hairs on the back of her neck bristled with primitive warning. She put her reaction down to nervousness. After all, she'd never been questioned by a policeman before, never even gotten a speeding ticket. Pleased at this rational explanation for her agitation, she turned and coolly inquired, "What was it you wanted, Detective Gallagher?"

"I don't know you well enough yet to tell you that!" The implication was unmistakable, but in case there was any doubt, his gaze boldly wandered across her body, visually stroking her with growing appreciation. "Ask me again in a week or two."

Now that they were up in the daylight, Amanda was able to see him properly. She already knew that his hair was dark and curly, but she discovered that his eyes were a warm molasses brown. His height was average, so that although he stood several inches taller than her five foot seven, he didn't tower over her. He was narrow-hipped, with the powerful shoulders of a swimmer. Dressed in the casual garb of a student — jeans, checked shirt, and down vest — there was little to indicate that Brady Gallagher was a police detective. The padding of his vest effectively hid the bulk of his shoulder holster in much the same way that Amanda suspected his teasing manner sheathed the strength of his will.

"Let me rephrase my question," Amanda stated silkily. "Did you wish to question me about the fire? If not, I have an incredible amount of work that I have to get back to."

Brady mockingly bowed his head. "As you so accurately guessed, I want to question you about the fire. Is there somewhere more private where we can discuss this?"

"We could go to my office."

"Fine. Lead the way."

Amanda regally did so, unaware of the provocative swing of her hips as she walked ahead of Brady. Her office, a mere cubbyhole separated from the other library offices by thin glass partitions, had two entrances. Today Amanda opted for the entrance in the hallway, preferring not to run the gauntlet of curious looks that walking through Technical Services would entail.

Brady made a point of holding the office door open for Amanda, motioning her through with a turn of his well-shaped hand. His fingers were long and tapered, his nails clean and short. All in all, it seemed a surprisingly sensitive hand for a policeman, and it momentarily had Amanda wondering what it would be like to have those hands touching her, caressing her. A fleeting image streaked across her mind, gone before it could be identified, but leaving behind a smoldering trail of perception.

Assuring herself that her interest was merely idle, Amanda brushed past Brady, noting the silver ID bracelet encompassing his left wrist as she did so. The cuffs of his checked shirt were folded back to reveal muscular forearms, hinting at the compact power of his build. Here was a man to be reckoned with.

Amanda continued on to her desk while Brady quickly surveyed his surroundings. In one glance he took in the framed Alpine poster, the rubber plant flourishing in the corner, and the brass nameplate on her desk. "Very nice, for a fishbowl. By the way, is this what you were looking for when you came sneaking down the stairs?"

"Thank you." Amanda took the inventory list he held out.

"Do you mind if I record our conversation?" he asked, setting a small cassette recorder on her desk before settling himself next to it.

"How come?"

Brady didn't bother looking up from adjusting the recorder. "How come what?"

Amanda eyed his downbent head in exasperation and resisted the temptation to test the texture of his hair by tugging on one of the dark coils that lay along the collar of his vest. "Why do you want to record this? Am I a suspect?"

"No, you're a possible witness."

"Aren't you supposed to read me my rights?" she challenged.

"Only if I'm going to book you." He paused,

tilting his head in a wry gesture of apology. “No pun intended.”

“All right.” With a graceful movement she sat down. “You can turn on the recorder.”

Brady did so, briefly identifying the conversation before asking, “What time did you discover the fire?”

“It was a little after one thirty.”

“How do you know? Did you stop and look at your watch?”

Amanda’s voice was coated with sarcasm. “No, I did not stop to check the time. I thought it more important to pull the fire alarm.”

“Then how do you know it was around one thirty?”

“Because I’d just gotten back from my lunch break and I always take it between twelve thirty and one thirty.”

“That’s good to know.” His murmured comment was too low for the recorder’s retrieval, but loud enough for her ears.

“Oh? Why’s that?” What bearing could her lunch hour habits have on this?

“In case I ever want to take you out for lunch.” Her eyes flicked up to his and caught him staring at her mouth as if he were contemplating making a meal of it. The sheer audacity of the man was overwhelming!

“How did you discover the fire?” he questioned, resuming the interrogation.

“I was going down to pull some material from the storage room.”

"Where were you coming from?"

"Here. My office."

"Did you notice anything unusual on your way down there?"

"Like someone carrying a flaming torch?" she inquired with saccharine sweetness, resenting his condescending tone.

"Why do I get the impression that you're trying to make things hard for me?" he mused.

"I can't imagine," Amanda tossed back.

"Did you notice anything out of the ordinary?"

"Besides the fire, you mean?"

Brady punched the cassette recorder's pause button with an exaggerated sigh. "Are you being deliberately perverse, or are you always this way?"

He was right. She shouldn't have been so flippant. Normally she wouldn't be, but something inside of her automatically responded to the challenge that was Brady Gallagher, bypassing her customary caution. "I'm sorry." Nodding his acceptance, Brady re-engaged the recorder as Amanda continued. "No, I didn't notice anything unusual."

"All right. What happened when you got down to the basement?"

"I smelled smoke. At first I thought some students had snuck down to grab a cigarette. There's no smoking allowed in the library," she explained parenthetically. "But it didn't quite smell like cigarette smoke, it was thicker. Then I noticed that the door to the storage room was ajar and I saw the flames inside."

"What did you do?"

"I ran upstairs, pulled the fire alarm, and got the students out of the stacks."

"But while you were in the basement you didn't see or hear anyone else?"

"No, I didn't. Why would someone set a fire down there?"

"That's what I'm trying to find out," Brady replied, turning off the recorder. "I'm going to have to question the rest of the library staff, and I think it might soothe their nerves if you were the one who told them about my interrogation."

Amanda led the way through a connecting door that led to the library's central processing area. "Could I have your attention, please?" was her request to the staff, who were no doubt already aware of Brady's presence if not his identity, since his dark head was clearly visible through the uncluttered panes of glass.

"This is Detective Gallagher from the Deerfield police department. He's here conducting an investigation into yesterday's fire and would like to speak to each of you. Please don't be concerned, this is a routine procedure and in no way signifies any suspicions of you."

"Thank you, Amanda," he warmly intoned.

She pivoted to glare at him, her stormy eyes silently questioning his right to use her first name. How had he known what it was anyway? She certainly hadn't told him. Enlightenment slowly dawned. The nameplate on her desk. The downward slant of Brady's eyes lent him a slumberous look that was deceptive, because this man certainly didn't miss a thing!

"I'd like to talk to each of you individually, if that's all right?" Brady requested with charm, showing none of the taunting mockery that he'd displayed with Amanda.

"Sure." It stood to reason that the eager agreement came from Susan, who had been eyeing Brady with predatory interest since he'd accompanied Amanda into the room. His answering grin further soured Amanda's already bad day.

"Is there someplace private where I could conduct the interrogations?" Brady turned to ask Amanda.

She bit back the sarcastic response she was so very tempted to give and instead directed him to a student conference room across the hallway. Susan, never one to be shy, was flirtatiously asking to be interrogated first when Amanda stalked back to her office.

Of course, given a choice, a man like Brady Gallagher was bound to give more attention to a curvacious twenty-year-old than to a grandmother like Helen. With the subject of age in mind, Amanda settled back in her office chair and momentarily wondered how old the police detective was. His casual attire made it difficult to pinpoint his age, but she'd guess him to be somewhere in his early thirties. *That's totally irrelevant,* an inner voice reprimanded. *Get back to work and stop this idle speculation.*

Amanda felt decidedly foolish for reacting so

vehemently to Brady Gallagher's flirtatious banter. She should have shrugged it off with a cool comment of her own, instead of continually rising to the bait as she had. If some part of her did long to indulge in the thrust and parry of verbal foreplay, it was kept well hidden under the visible professional image she displayed to the world at large.

Her blond good looks had always attracted male interest, but most men grew impatient with her cool self-possession and moved on to less challenging ground. Those men who did stick around treated her with a certain deference. Amanda, in turn, found their company amusing and pleasurable, but never disturbing.

Which brought her right back to Detective Gallagher. "Call me Brady," he'd instructed, probably an automatic reflex when faced with any woman under sixty. "Forget him," she muttered under her breath, reaching for the inventory list.

It would take her the better part of the afternoon to come up with cost and replacement estimates for the material lost in the fire. A shiver passed over her skin as she realized yet again how lucky they were that the fire had been contained. Despite Deerfield's reputation as a fine college, like so many other institutions of higher education it had its fair share of financial difficulties. Destruction of its impressive library collection would have been a major catastrophe.

Amanda had successfully relegated Brady

Gallagher to the back of her mind when, at four o'clock, she was interrupted by the entrance of a young man carrying a container of mums.

"I'm looking for Amanda Richards," he announced.

"I'm Amanda," she replied.

"Then these are for you. Please sign here." The young man held out a clipboard with a pen attached.

Assuming the flowers must be from Bob, her current escort, she signed on the allotted line. Beth came in the side door just as the delivery boy was leaving from the front.

"Here are those purchase orders you wanted from the acquisition files." She handed over the manila folders before exclaiming, "Flowers! Who are they from?"

"They're probably from Bob," Amanda replied absently, studying the contents of the folders.

"Funny," Beth mused. "Bob doesn't seem the type to send flowers. Here, there's a card attached."

Amanda opened the envelope Beth handed her to find a message written in an unfamiliar script. IT WOULD BE RIGHT IF YOU LEFT WITH ME TONIGHT. The card was unsigned. Only one man of her acquaintance would resort to such an errant pun.

"So, who are they from?" Beth prompted, her curiosity aroused.

"I don't have a clue," Amanda fibbed. "The card's unsigned." The intercom on her desk buzzed before Beth could press her further.

"Detective Gallagher for you on line one," the library secretary told her.

Amanda punched the appropriate button. "Yes, Detective Gallagher?"

"I thought I told you to call me Brady. Did you get my flowers?"

"Yes, Detective Gallagher," she replied, deliberately ignoring his directions.

"Am I calling you at a bad time or something?" he demanded, obviously picking up the cool dismissal of her tone.

"Yes." Amanda would have loved to have added "any time is a bad time" but was restrained by Beth's presence.

"Then I'll be brief. Come out to dinner with me tonight."

"No, Detective Gallagher. Thank you for calling. Good-bye."

"Hey, wait a minute!" he protested, but the rest was unintelligible as she hung up the phone.

"That was short," Beth noted from her position beside Amanda's desk. "I couldn't help but overhear you. What did he want?"

"Something he can't have!" Amanda snapped and then could have bitten off her tongue.

"Oh, ho. This sounds interesting! I want to hear all about it!"

"About what?" Amanda returned with feigned innocence.

"About you and Brady, of course."

"Don't be ridiculous. I hardly know the man."

Noting the militant look in Amanda's eyes, Beth beat a hasty retreat back to her own desk. Even though Amanda was a friend, she was also her boss and there was no mistaking that look of disapproval.

Amanda unlocked her front door with a tired sigh that evening. Walking into the living room she'd decorated herself right down to hanging the wallpaper, she kicked off her shoes and collapsed on the couch. She'd grown up in this house, slid down the wooden banister as a seven-year-old, sold lemonade on the front porch at eight, and fallen out of the oak tree out in back at nine. A lot of happy memories were enclosed within the two-story frame building, as well as a number of sad ones.

Since becoming a proud homeowner, Amanda had discovered that her desirability had soared with the eligible males in town. In these times of high interest rates, some men saw her as an attractive shortcut to owning a house. But not Bob Mason, a fellow homeowner. That was one of the reasons why she liked him, which reminded her that she'd better get dressed for their date tonight.

She was ready by the time Bob's car pulled into the driveway. Her glance in the mirror was an automatic reflex, for she already knew the silky plum dress looked good — it always did. Her hair was left loose, the honey-toned flicked-up tips falling with a planned naturalness that bespoke an excellent cut.

Bob took her to one of Deerfield's nicer restaurants, one not usually frequented by the student crowd. She was waiting in the foyer for Bob, who was parking the car, when a voice hailed her from behind. "Mandy!" No one had called her that since the orthodontist had removed her braces! She turned to find Brady standing behind her.

"I almost didn't recognize you with your hair down," he mocked.

"Nor I you, without your vest," she shot back. The only concession he'd made to the restaurant's dress code was to replace his vest with a navy blue blazer. His muscular legs were still encased in their form-fitting jeans.

"Aren't you going to introduce me, Amanda?" Bob inserted, walking in on the tail end of their conversation.

"Of course. This is Detective Gallagher. Bob Mason."

Bob thrust out his hand in a reluctant manner, wincing at Brady's unnecessarily firm grip. "Detective Gallagher," he acknowledged briefly.

"Call me Brady." The words may have been spoken to Bob, but the intent was directed at Amanda.

Bob placed a proprietorial arm around Amanda's waist and said, "Our table's ready. Excuse us, Brady."

"Of course," Brady nodded, waving them along. "Enjoy your meal."

Amanda was still fuming over Brady's use of the nickname "Mandy" while Bob helped her into her seat. Thank heaven Bob hadn't overheard that!

"Everything all right?" he questioned, sitting down across from her.

"Fine. Why do you ask?"

"You looked a little disturbed."

Amanda could well imagine. Unfortunately she had the type of complexion that reflected her emotions, going from pale alabaster when she was tired or anxious, to a flushed rosiness when she was angry or embarrassed. At thirty she should be well past blushing, but since she hadn't outgrown the involuntary trait by now, there was little hope of it disappearing.

"It's been a rough day," she belatedly answered Bob.

Somehow it got rougher when she looked up and saw Brady accompanying a gorgeous redhead into the dining room. So much for his being crushed by her refusal to have dinner with him! Bob's voice calling her name brought her attention back to him.

"I asked if you were ready to order."

"Not yet." Amanda bent her head to study the menu, but was hard-pressed to find something appetizing. Her disinterest in food had nothing to do with the restaurant's notable cuisine; it was entirely due to Brady's inhibiting presence. Even though a roomful of diners separated them, she was still very much aware of him.

During the course of their meal, Amanda really tried to concentrate her attention on Bob. In his late thirties, he was a successful accountant who had his own practice. With one broken marriage behind him, he was not about to rush into anything the second time around. That innate caution was what had first attracted Amanda to him.

Of course it stood to reason that they ran into Brady again on their way out. He was turning from the bar, drink in hand, when he almost collided with Bob, whose attention was focused on Amanda.

"Excuse me." Bob automatically apologized.

"It's quite all right." With devilish amusement Brady's eyes narrowed in on Amanda's hand clinging to Bob's arm. "It's hard to concentrate when Mandy's hands are all over you."

Her shocked "Brady!" coincided exactly with Bob's stunned "Mandy?"

Brady viewed their differing reactions with unconvincing bewilderment. "Did I say something wrong?"

Brady's little-boy expression made Amanda long to kick him. Instead she had to satisfy herself with a curt, "Yes."

Brady elected to ignore her, turning to Bob and confiding with man-to-man candor, "I've warned her about such abandoned behavior. All I can say is that she's lucky I'm a cop. God only knows what kind of trouble she could've gotten herself into otherwise." A shake of his head was meant to mark his masculine concern.

Amanda's protest was immediate. "You're making it sound like I was hustling on street corners!"

Brady had the gall to laugh. "A librarian? You've gotta be kidding! Besides, I don't work in vice."

"Neither do I!" she shot back icily before turning on her heels and stalking out of the restaurant, followed by a perturbed Bob.

"What was all that about?" he demanded.

"Nothing," she snapped, residual anger still coloring her voice.

"You didn't react as if it were nothing. Where did you meet that guy?"

"Detective Gallagher is investigating the fire we had at work," Amanda explained briefly. "Without knowing who he was, I called college security on him when I found him in a restricted area."

"What does this have to do with his suggestive insinuations?"

"The guard wanted to see Brady's ID before he'd let him go."

"You mean Gallagher was forcibly detained?"

"One way of putting it, yes." Amanda sighed impatiently. Bob certainly had a way with words. "The guard asked me to get Brady's wallet, that's all."

Bob shook his head in amazement. "Who would've thought that working in a library would be so exciting?"

Coming from some, the comment would have been a teasing remark, but from Bob it was an expression of genuine disbelief. In his eyes libraries were still hallowed shrines where wizened men and women bent over illuminated manuscripts! He had no concept of the complicated computerized systems that operated a modern-day learning research center.

In the week following the fire it seemed to Amanda that Brady was going out of his way to irritate her. Mocking glances, teasing inflections, and a suggestive attitude were all part of his combat kit. It didn't help matters any that Susan and most of the other female members of the library staff talked about him continually, dreamily noting every one of his physical attributes and speculating on his sexual prowess. In a bid to retain her sanity, Amanda took to spending more time outside of her office, dealing with inter-administrative matters. Upon her return from a meeting in the business office, Amanda was informed of yet another visit by the infuriating detective.

"Amanda, where were you? Detective Gallagher was looking for you a while ago," Beth chattered.

Amanda sent a hurried glance around the processing room, as if suspecting that Brady was hiding behind one of the desks, before answering in what she hoped was a dispassionate manner. "Oh?"

Beth nodded excitedly. "He said there was no message, but that he would try again later."

"Great!" Amanda muttered under her breath, walking through to her own office and dumping the pile of computer printouts she'd borrowed from the business office on her desk.

"I've got to collect some statistics from Government Documents to add to our budget justification."

Beth smiled knowingly. "What should I tell Brady if he comes looking for you."

"Tell him . . ." Amanda changed the fiery destination she had in mind and took a deep breath before calmly continuing. "Tell him to wait here in my office. I won't be gone long."

The government documents office was located down the hallway and to the right. Walking past rows of bookshelves, Amanda was unaware of what an attractive picture she presented, her honey gold hair gathered up away from her face. The severe style revealed her fine features, throwing her high cheekbones and wide brown eyes into prominence. Her creamy butter-colored blouse was tucked into the trim skirt of her russet suit. More than one masculine pair of eyes were momentarily distracted from the printed lines of their textbooks.

As luck would have it, the document listing the statistics she needed was sitting on the top shelf. Noting the column of ants trooping across the metal support brackets, Amanda made a mental note to call Physical Plant about pest control. The subject of pest control brought Brady Gallagher to mind.

The next time they met she was determined to maintain total composure. Standing on a step stool, one nylon-clad leg stretched out behind her for balance, she didn't bother turning around when she heard the sound of approaching footsteps. Assuming it was Beth, Amanda brashly inquired, "Has the pest left yet?" It was an inadvertent lapse, a sort of Freudian slip, but Beth would understand.

Brady did not. "You wouldn't be talking about me now, would you, Mandy?" his deep voice shot back.

Chapter Two

The sight of him unbalanced her, both figuratively and literally. Amanda grabbed wildly, trying to catch something to prevent her fall. Instead, something caught her. Brady's strong hands gripped her waist, his fingers firm and sure as he lowered her to the floor before him.

Amanda's momentary feelings of foolishness were swamped by a more powerful pull. Her eyes were caught up in the rich brown of Brady's gaze, her nostrils filled with the clean freshness of his masculine scent, her soul was shaken by her subliminal recognition of his touch. A current of sexual awareness was coursing its way through her, the electricity originating from his hands spanning her waist. His fingertips were resting in the sensitive hollow of her spine, his thumbs splayed across the smooth curve of her stomach. The silky thinness of her blouse only served to intensify the erotic stimulation of the moment.

The spell was finally broken by Brady's dry observation. "I suppose this is an example of eavesdroppers hearing no good of themselves."

"I'm sorry," Amanda murmured huskily, willing the bumpy unevenness of her heart to stop. She felt like an absolute idiot! So much for her hopes of maintaining the upper hand in their next confrontation. Thinking of hands made her wonder how his would feel against the bare warmth of her skin, traveling the hidden byways of her body. Her mental image of such a situation left her momentarily speechless.

"Am I forgiven for my scurrilous statements at the restaurant last week?" Brady inquired, noting her heightened color with interest.

"Of course," she managed to answer, relieved to feel his grip loosen before he let her go.

"Funny. That's not the impression you've been giving. In fact, I've gotten the distinct feeling that we've been playing a little game of hide-and-seek for the past week. With you hiding and me seeking!"

"And just what are you seeking, Brady?" Amanda demanded, stepping away from him, needing to put some space between herself and the powerful magnetism of his captivating smile. A little healthy indignation might be just the thing to cure this sudden attack of attraction, she decided.

Brady eyed her with mocking amusement before answering, "I would've thought that was obvious. I want you to come out with me. To prove that there are no hard feelings."

"Thanks, but no thanks."

"What's the matter?" he gently taunted. "Scared?"

"Of you? No!" Her denial was firmly emphatic.

"Then prove it," he challenged. "Or do I have

to submit a financial report before you accept dates?"

Clearly he was aware of Bob's successful status in life. The possibility of Brady suffering from envy was somehow cheering; it meant that his self-confidence wasn't dent-proof. That supposition brought a smile to Amanda's lips and a playful jauntiness to her words. "No, a financial report isn't necessary, but a character reference might be nice."

She'd meant it as a joke, but Brady turned the tables on her. "Fine. How many references would you like?" he asked, as if this were a request he was often called upon to supply.

He had to be kidding, didn't he? Masking her confusion, Amanda smoothly replied, "Two should be sufficient."

"No problem. See you later," and with a wave of his hand he was gone.

He really was the most impossible man! Appealing, but still impossible! He'd probably only been pulling her leg, although she couldn't imagine why he got such a kick out of irritating her. His presence had sharpened her appetite as well as her mind, simultaneously making both her heart and her thoughts race faster. *That's adrenaline, not sex appeal!* she tried to convince herself with an impatient shake of her head.

It didn't work. There was no getting around it. This was definitely sex appeal, this strange tugging need that left a hungry ache in its wake. *So what are you going to do about it?* an inner voice mocked. "Not a damn thing!" Amanda answered out loud.

She returned to her office to find Guy Lox, a professor in the Natural Science Department, waiting for her. He was her least favorite person on campus, thoroughly aggravating. Aggravating, however, in a different way from Brady. Even though the latter frequently infuriated her, he did have a lot of good points. Guy had none.

Guy's face was unmemorable, the features seemingly having been picked at random and stuck together in one place. He had a short, stocky figure that was habitually garbed in mismatched and ill-fitting clothes. Unappealing though he was, Guy Lox was a powerful member of the library faculty committee and therefore someone she couldn't afford to offend.

Today he'd stopped by to drop off a pile of requests for books he wanted ordered. Amanda would have been more tolerant had his collection development plans been serious, but they invariably already owned 98 percent of the titles he wanted while the other two percent were so far out as to be laughable. Case in point, his request for a book on a tuna psychology workshop!

"Ah, Amanda, these book requests were piling up on my desk," Guy pompously reported. "And as I have so many other important things to finish before the weekend, I thought I'd get them out of my way."

"Thank you," she said insincerely.

"Not at all," he responded with lordly graciousness. "What are your plans for the weekend?" Guy had been trying to finagle a date with her since he'd first started teaching at the college.

"I'm going to be very busy." Amanda had honed her evasions to a fine art.

Guy responded to her no-nonsense tone by changing the subject. "I'm attending a meeting this afternoon with the dean. You know" — he lowered his voice confidentially — "I think he might appoint me to the next vacancy on the tenure committee. We see eye-to-eye on administrative matters and he often asks me for my advice."

Guy was totally involved in climbing the internal ladder of success and consequently was often in the middle of a number of Machiavellian plots and power plays. Amanda personally thought that a better appearance and a nicer disposition would gain Guy a lot more than the kind of backstabbing he seemed to enjoy participating in. But that was his problem; she had enough of her own to contend with.

The following week was very hectic. Two members of the library support staff quit, so they were now shorthanded. On Wednesday the circulation librarian called in sick, which meant that the remaining librarians had to rotate hourly shifts at the reference desk out in the main reading room. Amanda spent her hour alternating between helping bewildered students find information and reprimanding others for sneaking cups of coffee into the library. Although NO DRINKING, EATING, OR SMOKING signs were prominently displayed throughout, Amanda still caught at least half a dozen people trying to enter with containers of coffee or lit cigarettes.

After firmly repeating the rules so many times, she began to feel like a law enforcement officer. Most of the students were pleasant about it, but there's always one in every crowd who won't comply without a fight.

"Where's it say there's no drinking?" one belligerent girl demanded.

Amanda pointed to the sign right behind her.

"Well, I've never heard of such an idiotic rule."

"All libraries have that rule to protect their books from accidents," Amanda patiently explained. "The replacement cost for damaged books has risen dramatically over the past few years."

"I've always brought in coffee and never been stopped before. I'm not a kindergartener who's going to spill everything all over my books!"

"The rule stands. If you like, you can speak to the head librarian about it." This tactic proved successful in getting the student to bad-naturedly give in, throwing her full cup into the trash, muttering under her breath all the while. Given the choice, few people wanted to talk to John Abbington, and Amanda couldn't really blame them.

"Any time you want to apply for a position down at the police station, just give me a call," a masculine voice drawled.

Amanda whirled around. "Brady!" How did

he always manage to sneak up on her?

"No more Detective Gallagher, I see. That *is* an improvement." Brady congratulated Amanda with a grin that was ever so slightly lopsided.

"What are you doing here?" she asked, noting the envelope he held in his hand.

"I've got something for you." He dropped the envelope on top of the desk.

"What's this?"

"My references," Brady solemnly replied. "Aren't you going to open it?"

Amanda cautiously did so, as if fearing the contents might bite her. Her fingers alighted on an innocuous sheet of paper, which she pulled out and read.

> "Dear Amanda. It's about time someone asked for references from a sister — no one's ever had the good sense to consult me before. Brady is pretty nice, considering he's an older brother. You can't expect too much from them, can you? Although Brady tends to be overprotective, you shouldn't run into any problems. Don't play Monopoly with him though. He'll accuse you of cheating if you win! Good luck! Ginny Gallagher."

Amanda had to laugh. "Your sister's editorial commentary is most enlightening!"

Brady leaned forward, bracing his hands palm down on the desk that separated them. "My sister does cheat at Monopoly," he maintained, studying her mouth with a sensual absorption that Amanda found very disturbing.

Running the tip of her tongue around her suddenly parched lips, she launched into nervous conversation. "Did you know that Monopoly was invented by a University of Wisconsin graduate?"

"Don't change the subject," he chided, lifting his gaze to her eyes.

"I wasn't," she denied. "You brought up Monopoly and I was just . . ."

"I know exactly what you were trying to do," Brady interrupted, watching her smooth back her hair in an agitated gesture. "So? Did I pass the inspection? If not, there's another reference in the envelope that confirms my skill in . . ." His pause was deliberate. ". . . certain specialized activities."

Amanda dropped the envelope as if burned. She had no doubts about what kind of activities he was referring to and she had no intention of reading a resume of his sexual activities. Brady's amusement was evident. In fact he seemed to be having a hard time restraining outright laughter.

Amanda could feel fury stealing her patience. Since Brady found her to be such an entertaining diversion, the obvious solution was to give him an evening so boring that he'd give up in desperation, that is if he didn't fall asleep first! "There's a concert at eight o'clock tomorrow night at the college auditorium." She deliberately made her voice sound hesitant, knowing that he'd assume it was a rock concert, as was the norm.

An unsuspecting Brady immediately said, "Sounds great! What time shall I pick you up?"

"That's all right," she hedged. "I'll meet you at the auditorium." Her plan didn't call for her being dependent upon him for a ride home, because there was no telling what kind of mood he'd be in by the time she was done with him!

"Amanda, I know where you live, it's right on my way home. We'd save gas if I picked you up and dropped you off afterward."

Unable to fight such energy-efficient logic, Amanda reluctantly agreed.

"Great." He abandoned his slanted pose over the desk. "See you at seven tomorrow night."

Amanda spent the afternoon bent over a pile of accounts payable printouts, determined to clean up the duplicate billing problem they'd encountered with one of their many vendors. This sort of mixup made her even more determined to consolidate jobbers. While reaching across her desk for a folder, she inadvertently upended the envelope containing Brady's references, spilling its contents onto the printouts.

Along with his sister's letter there was a round cloth patch attached to a sheet of paper. She picked it up, gazing in amused astonishment at the boy scout badge nestled in the palm of her hand. It had indeed been awarded for skill in a specialized activity — signaling. How appropriate! "An old skill that can be fun," the accompanying tip sheet explained.

"Tonight, Brady Gallagher, you're going to get your signals crossed!" Amanda murmured in what could easily have been mistaken for gleeful anticipation.

It was no surprise that Brady arrived at her doorstep on time, and his attire was as casual as she'd expected. A madras plaid shirt was tucked into his form-fitting jeans while a brown leather belt hugged his lean waist, its intricate silver buckle drawing and holding her attention until modesty moved her eyes elsewhere. Proceeding upward, Amanda deliberately avoided his face and the snaring pools of his eyes. Instead, she focused on the thick curly mane of his dark hair, noting the way it conformed to the shape of his head, brushing the back of his collar, unaccountably making her long to run her fingers through it. His blazer was the same one he'd worn that night at the restaurant, when he'd embarrassed her in front of Bob, and the memory strengthened her resolve to repay him in kind.

Meanwhile Brady was undertaking a study of his own. He quickly noted, although he made no comment on, the expensive simplicity of her dress. His innate suspicion made him question her sophisticated appearance, but he chalked it up to her natural elegance and paused to appreciate the overall effect of clinging jersey and nylon-sheathed legs. Unknowingly he pursed his lips in a silent whistle before he asked, "You ready?"

At Amanda's nod Brady stepped forward to

assist her with her coat. He then reached out to gently free her golden hair from its subsequent imprisonment beneath the collar of her coat. The feel of his hands on her nape induced a now familiar surge of excitement, an electrifying shiver that danced over her. There it was again, what the song writers so lyrically called "black magic." Determined not to become a victim, Amanda quickly moved away.

Outside, the night air held a promise of frost as they rustled through the dried leaves on the sidewalk. Brady generously offered his assistance, asking her if she needed help raking the colorful offerings.

"No, thanks. The boy next door would be brokenhearted if you stole his job. Work's hard to find in a college town, especially if you're only eleven!"

"Far be it from me to condemn an eleven-year-old to the breadlines," Brady laughed as he opened the passenger door of his car.

It wasn't until Amanda was inside that she realized what kind of car it was, an unmarked patrol car. "This is a police car!" she accused Brady as soon as he slid behind the wheel.

"Then aren't you lucky that a police officer is driving it, otherwise you'd be in real trouble," he mocked.

"Don't you have a car of your own?"

"What's wrong? Afraid I'm too broke to pay for tonight's tickets?" he mocked in return, avoiding her question.

"I can pay for my own ticket tonight," she offered. It really wouldn't be fair to expect him to pay for both of their tickets, since he was bound to hate the concert anyway.

"No way, Mandy. I invited you, I'll pay. By the way, I never got a chance to check. What group's playing tonight?"

"It's a surprise. And Brady, I'd rather you didn't call me Mandy."

"Why not?"

"Because it isn't suitable."

"Suitable?" Brady tossed back his head with a shout of laughter that made Amanda grip her purse in indignant frustration. How dare he laugh at her!

Sensing her anger, Brady tried to restrain himself. "I'm sorry, Mandy, but if you could've heard the way you sounded."

"Don't apologize," she purred. "It's my pleasure to provide amusement for you."

"Amusement isn't the only thing I'd like you to provide," he huskily imparted. "And as for your pleasure . . ."

"Shouldn't you keep your mind on your driving," she reprimanded with gentle firmness.

Mandell Hall was the central hub in a wheel of buildings, with radiating walkways forming concrete spokes. Amanda had not anticipated that such a large crowd would be attending the concert. She and Brady walked into the auditorium foyer with a group of other people who blocked the evening's program posters from Brady's eyes. It wasn't until they filed down the center aisle that he became aware of what was in store for him.

The stage did not hold large amplifying speakers or microphones as it would have had this been a standard rock concert. Instead it was set up with alternating, semi-circular rows of empty chairs and music stands. Some of the musicians had already begun to assemble and were tuning up their instruments.

Brady accepted the pair of programs from the student usher and turned to hand Amanda hers with a speaking look. "Some surprise, Mandy."

"Don't you like classical music, Brady?" she questioned, borrowing his pseudoinnocent expression.

"We'll have to wait and see, won't we," he murmured as they sat down.

Anticipating his upcoming discomfort, Amanda's lips formed an unsuccessfully hidden grin. She didn't think she'd have any more trouble with Detective Brady Gallagher after this evening!

Brady noticed her grin, and could easily guess the reasons for it. He also noticed the appearance of a dimple that flashed at the corner of her mouth. Confident of his ability to handle her, he didn't really blame Amanda for her scheme. He'd always appreciated a challenge!

The lights lowered and the audience applauded the guest conductor's entrance from the side of the stage. Shortly thereafter the melodious strains of "The Moldau" filled the air.

As the musical program continued, Amanda was

disconcerted to observe that Brady showed no signs of restlessness. He sat relaxed in his seat, not fidgeting, not even toying with his program. His fingers weren't drumming impatiently on the armrest and he hadn't fallen asleep. This was not going according to plan. He wasn't supposed to enjoy the concert!

"How do you like it so far?" she asked at the intermission, hoping that he'd voice his boredom.

"Very evocative," was his astounding response.

"You mean you liked it?"

"Wasn't I supposed to?" he challenged, notifying her that he knew about her plan.

"I don't know what that's supposed to mean," she prevaricated.

"Don't you?" he murmured softly.

It took a great deal of effort to disentangle herself from the intimate mockery of his ensnaring gaze. Amanda had to consciously jerk her eyes away and direct them toward the program her fingers were nervously dog-earing. Unnerved by her undoubted vulnerability, she launched into speech. "They'll be playing Tchaikovsky's *Capriccio Italien* after the intermission," *which had better be over soon,* she silently continued.

"The program here says that it was written in one week. Amazing what can be accomplished in such a short span of time, isn't it?" Brady was saying one thing while talking about another, no mean accomplishment. It required an expressive voice, something he definitely possessed. He could project a caressing warmth into his pitch, add a dash of light mockery to an inflection, or deepen his timbre to a husky admonition.

"Have you lived in Deerfield long?" Amanda inquired, fighting the spell he was weaving.

"I was born here," he replied, which didn't really answer her question. "How about you?"

"Same here." If he could be evasive, so could she!

"It's strange we never met before."

"Not really," she dismissed. "I haven't had much contact with the police."

"That's reassuring to hear." Brady lowered his head to confide, "You'd be amazed how many women want to have a lot of 'contact' with the police."

Amanda's startled gaze slid over his face, which was deadpan with the exception of the slightest twinge at the very corner of his surprisingly curvaceous lips. Amanda recognized that telltale sign as an expression of his mocking humor. Goodness knows she'd seen Brady wearing it often enough when dealing with her. That's what had gotten her ire up in the first place, down in the basement of the library when he'd invited her to frisk him. Amanda wasn't accustomed to being laughed at, and she still wasn't sure she liked it.

"I'm sure your training helps you cope with their attentions," she mocked in return, her eyes emphasizing the point.

"Which training might that be?"

"Combat training, of course."

"Of course," he grinned.

During the second part of the program Amanda displayed all the signs of restlessness that she'd hoped to inflict on Brady. Instead, here she was, herself the victim.

The situation did not please her one bit. Bored with the orchestra before her, she let the force of the music carry her thoughts away. But that proved to be a dangerous exercise, for Brady played a major role in those thoughts.

Sensory impressions of him flashed on the screen of her mind, impressions that she couldn't block out although she gave it a good try. The cool cotton of his shirt compared to the warm skin it covered, the tempting touch of his hands on her waist, the devilish promise in his dark eyes; all these things, and many more, came to mind. Bob had never bothered her to this degree, had never interfered with her thought processes.

A round of applause jerked her back to reality. Amanda joined in the audience's appreciation, even though she hadn't paid much attention to the orchestra's performance. Brady's enthusiastic clapping didn't improve her humor any. Did he have to look so relaxed, so at ease? Didn't he realize he was supposed to feel out of place? Instead, here she was, feeling out of sorts.

The drive back to her house was done to the accompaniment of the car's police band radio. The gravelly noise made her think she had inadvertently stumbled into a *Police Story* episode, and she fully expected it to be interrupted by a commercial at any moment. Brady pulled the car in front of her darkened house with a smoothness that denoted confident control. The porch light was on, illuminating the path up to the front entrance.

"You don't have to escort me all the way to the door," she protested as Brady unfastened his safety belt.

"I know I don't have to, but I want to."

Amanda knew what was coming before he stopped at the door and leaned his dark head toward her. Tension flooded over her, and defenses were automatically employed. Brady wouldn't have been human if he hadn't noticed the change.

"Relax!" His reassuring voice was tinged with exasperation. "I'm not going to attack you, Mandy. Just kiss you good night."

There was no way of explaining that it wasn't him she was afraid of, but herself. Steeling herself to remain calm and impassive, Amanda prepared to coolly accept his kiss. Brady lowered his head with unhurried deliberation. His lips got as close as they could without actually touching hers. Amanda found the evocative proximity nerve-racking, and it required all her powers of resistance to stave off the trembling weakness of her limbs.

Just when she thought she couldn't resist the temptation a moment longer, he slowly pulled away to place a chaste kiss on her forehead. Viewing her evident surprise, Brady accounted for his restraint. "Isn't that how a librarian expects to be kissed?"

Nothing he could have said would have angered her more or made her more determined to prove him wrong. Which is, of course, why he'd said it in the first place! Amanda, who had heard this approach before, decided to give Brady enough rope to hang himself.

"Librarians do not kiss any differently from other women," she snapped, getting into her role of a woman insulted.

"Really?" Brady's voice held just the right amount of calculated doubt.

"You sound unconvinced," she purred.

He made matters worse by explaining, "It's the cop in me. I only go on facts, not on wild claims."

Really, Brady was asking for it, and Amanda considered herself woman enough to give it to him! "Would you consider an example as admissible evidence?"

"That's all right, Mandy," he excused with condescending generosity. "I realize it would be hard for you."

"Let me worry about that," she sweetly commanded, raising her arms to clasp them around his neck.

Brady stood before her, outwardly unmoved by the feel of her soft body pressed against his. But inside he was experiencing the first twinges of doubt about the wisdom of this little game. Amanda Richards had raised his blood pressure since the first time she'd placed her investigating fingers in his pants pocket searching for his ID.

Now that he'd spent some time with her, he knew that that first ember of attraction burned deep. But she was so damned stubborn at times that he couldn't resist taunting her. At the moment though, his protective instincts were telling him that he was about to get more than he'd bargained for!

Amanda could discern none of those thoughts from Brady's impassive expression. Stung by his apparent unresponsiveness, she sliced her fingers through the coiled strands of dark hair that curled over his collar, her nails lightly raking his scalp. Her hand then moved to cup his ear, amplifying the sound of his name on her lips. Soft puffs of her minty breath baited him, tying him in knots.

"This is how librarians kiss," she murmured against his mouth.

Intent on having the last laugh, Amanda brought all her knowledge and a dash of imagination into play. Her tongue lightly surveyed the unfamiliar contour of his lips, which were surprisingly soft and firm. Unaccustomed to being the aggressor, she was unprepared for the heady sense of power that shot through her. Encouraged, she boldly pressed on, deepening the pressure of the kiss.

The initiative passed back and forth as Brady responded to her play. His mouth opened, releasing his own tongue, which was eager to mate with hers. One hand tunneled under her hair to hold her just so, the slanting angle of the contact ensuring maximum pleasure as he drank in the nectar of her essence.

His arms engulfed her slowly, binding her to him. Amanda found herself pressing against a masculine body that was as compactly powerful as she'd suspected. A coil of longing unfurled itself deep within her, laying her prey to its primal message. Her fingers registered his thermal warmth as they slipped around his waist and kneaded the muscles of his tapered back.

When Brady finally tore his mouth from hers it was to hoarsely mutter, "God, you're wonderful!"

The lesson had gone further than she'd expected and her response had subsequently gone deeper. It took a concentrated effort to remember that it was all playacting. Or so it was supposed to be. Gathering her shattered composure, she unsteadily inquired, "Is that an admission that you're a bad judge of character?"

"No. I knew . . ." he began, concentrating more on threading his fingers through the incredible softness of her hair than on the possible effects of his admission.

She felt his body tense in anticipation of her fury. But instead of throwing a fit, Amanda continued to confound him by huskily prompting, "Did you enjoy the kiss?"

Triumphant victory flashed across his face, coloring his voice. "I enjoyed it very much, Mandy," he husked, reaching out to pull her closer.

Twisting out of his embrace, Amanda deployed her verbal assault with a tart, "I sincerely hope you did, because that's the only one you'll ever get from me!" She whirled to slam the door in Brady's astonished face.

His taunting voice followed her upstairs. "Don't make promises you can't keep, Mandy!"

Chapter Three

Amanda had spent a restless night, punching her pillow at assorted intervals, and wishing it could have been a certain impossible policeman she was attacking instead of the defenseless feathers. Her temper did not improve once she got to work and faced a barrage of questions from her curious coworkers.

The first one came before she'd even gotten to her office as the registrar stopped her on the front steps. "I hear you and a certain police detective were spotted mingling at a popular nightspot last night," the other woman chirped in the tone of a Hollywood gossip columnist.

"If you would call listening to a classical concert mingling, and Mandell Hall as a popular nightspot, then I suppose what you heard was correct," Amanda breezily retorted before continuing on her way up the stairs.

The next question came while Amanda was pouring herself a cup of coffee from the library's community pot. "Did you have a nice time last night?" Helen asked with motherly concern.

Nice was not the word Amanda would have used to describe her evening. Frustrating, infuriating, surprising, all came closer to the truth. So did enchanting. The kiss they'd shared was pure, unadulterated magic, a double-edged sword that was reason enough not to see Brady Gallagher again, but powerful enough to ensure that she would.

"Amanda?" Helen's voice pulled her back to the present.

"Yes, Helen, I had a nice time," she belatedly replied.

Surprisingly Beth remained silent, but that was merely because she planned on cornering Amanda at lunch. Since it was a perfect Indian summer day they spent their lunch hour down by the lake, sitting on one of the many benches dotting the grassy edges.

"All right, Amanda." Beth paused to open up her lunch bag. "What gives?"

Popping the top of her Tupperware container, Amanda feigned ignorance. "What are you talking about?"

"Come on. What's really going on between you and Brady Gallagher?"

"There's nothing going on." Amanda dismissed her question, taking a bite of her salad.

Beth was undeterred. "He sent you flowers last week and now he's dating you."

"We attended one concert together. That's not dating!"

"How did you know that Brady would like classical music?" Beth asked, lifting the lid off her yogurt container.

"I didn't," Amanda let slip.

"But what if he hadn't liked it?" One look

at Amanda's guilty expression confirmed Beth's niggling suspicions. "I see."

Amanda jabbed a piece of lettuce with her plastic fork, refusing to comment on her friend's enlightenment.

"That wasn't real bright, Amanda."

"I know. He enjoyed the concert more than I did."

"Serves you right."

"Hey! Whose side are you on?"

"Side? Now this is getting interesting. Sounds like a war!"

"Can we change the subject?" Amanda requested.

Their conversation swung back to work and the ongoing complaints about the head librarian's competence, or lack of it. "You know that report you completed on the material damaged in the fire. Would you believe Abbington had the gall to tell the dean that he had prepared that report himself?"

Amanda muttered something under her breath. She'd have to have another little talk with John, whose imminent retirement was the only thing that saved him from a more public exposure. As it was, the dean already knew that Amanda had written the report, since she'd spoken to him about it before turning it over to John, a safety precaution on her part. Amanda had worked hard to get where she was, and she had every intention of winning the appointment of head librarian once John left.

Amanda's day didn't improve, as the first person to greet her upon her return to the library was Guy Lox.

"Amanda, I've been waiting for you," he rebuked impatiently, following her into her office.

"You should've left a message, Professor. I know how valuable your time is."

Not hearing the veiled mockery in her voice, Guy preened under the compliment. "That's true, but I wanted to know if that book on insect mutations has come in yet."

"No, it hasn't." The book had been ordered against her better judgment, but she'd been overruled by John. "We'll send you a memo when it arrives."

"I hear you're seeing a lot of our undercover detective." Guy's voice was heavy with disapproving innuendo.

"He's not undercover," Amanda denied, ignoring the sexual intent of Guy's statement.

"That was a little joke," Guy leaned closer to explain with a disgusting leer.

"Very little," Brady volunteered from the threshold. His laughing eyes watched the other man straighten up with a speed that was ludicrous.

"I must be going," Guy muttered, cautiously veering around the motionless, jean-clad menace of the detective before making a quick getaway.

Brady shook his head in laughing disbelief. "Who was that little man?"

"Professor Guy Lox, Natural Science Department," Amanda briefly listed.

"Figures."

"What can I do for you, Detective?"

Amanda's voice was coolly professional; Brady's response was not. "Nothing that can be done in this office."

It wasn't only what Brady said, but the way he said it that was equally disturbing. "This suggestive banter may be your idea of a good time," she shot back, "but I've got more important things to do."

"Now, Mandy, don't get on your high horse. I need to talk to you."

"I think we pretty well covered everything last night, Detective Gallagher."

"On the contrary. But that's a different matter. Right now I'd like to talk to you about the fire."

"Oh." She felt rather foolish for assuming Brady had come to discuss last night, when in fact it was an official visit.

Brady pulled the visitor's chair right up to her desk before sitting down. Suddenly the desk was transformed from a barrier to a working surface to be shared. He pulled a small notebook and a cassette recorder out of his vest pocket.

Amanda was beginning to know his clothes almost as well as she did her own. That vest was the same one that she'd fumbled under the first time she'd met him, his shirt in muted grays and blues, the same one that he'd worn the day he'd shown her his "references," and the jeans hugging the male symmetry of his body were identical to the ones he'd worn last night.

"Mandy?" His voice asked for her attention.

"Mmm?" She'd given up trying to talk him out of using that nickname. In fact, the way he said it, it sounded kind of nice — warm and special. *Wait a minute, what's wrong with you?* she silently demanded. *This man is dangerous, he proved it last night!*

All he did was kiss you, her sense of fair play contradicted. *He wanted you in his arms and he got you there. And you enjoyed it too, didn't you?*

"Amanda!" That did get her attention.

"I'm sorry. I was thinking about something."

"Something, or someone?" he challenged. The conflict in her eyes hadn't gone unnoticed by him. Brady caught that certain look and was willing to bet that a man had put it there. Had she been thinking about Bob Mason? The possibility irritated him.

What the hell was he worrying about it for anyway? He was here to discuss the fire. The past two weeks had turned up nothing in the way of clues about the arsonist's identity. The lab report had come back with no conclusive results, except for the matter he'd come to discuss with Mandy.

"The day you discovered the fire, you told me you'd gone downstairs to get some material out of the storage room."

"That's correct."

"What kind of material?"

"Duplicate books and periodicals. We participate in a duplicate exchange program with other libraries, trading our extra copies for things we need."

"Okay, so what happened when you got downstairs?"

"Happened?"

Brady rephrased his question. "What did you see?"

"I didn't see very much. As you know the lighting down there is not the best. I did smell smoke though, as I told you before."

Brady checked his notebook where he'd outlined the critical points of their last taped conversation. "Go on," he prompted.

"The smoke was coming from the storage room and I could see flames through the open door."

This was what he'd been hoping for! "You're sure the door was already open when you got downstairs?"

"Yes."

"Is that door normally left open?"

"No, normally it's locked."

"Who had keys to the room?"

"I did, as did every department head. Then there's one copy kept up front at the reference desk."

Brady swore under his breath. "So anyone could have had access to a key. Why was the room kept locked? Were any of the materials stored there valuable?"

"No. The few rare books we have are kept

in a fireproof file in the archive room. The storage room was kept locked only to prevent vandalism."

Brady jumped on that. "Had there been any trouble with the storage room before? Any attempts to break into it, anything like that?"

"No, none at all that I'm aware of. You might want to check with Security to see if they had any reports."

Brady reached out a hand to switch off the pocket-sized cassette recorder and wrote a few lines in his notebook. But it was the way he wrote them that caught Amanda's attention. She watched the telltale hook of his left hand as he scribbled down a few more notes before closing the pad. Why hadn't she noticed before?

"You're left-handed!"

"That's right," he acknowledged with what sounded like a small degree of defensiveness.

Amanda couldn't resist the temptation to tease him, as he so often did her. "No, that's not right. That's left." Her rose-tipped finger reached out to tap his other hand. "This one is right."

"So you do know your left from your right!" he mused in apparent amazement.

"Of course I do," she returned.

"Then you must have been deliberately playing around under my vest." He grinned expectantly, anticipating her display of outrage.

But Amanda wasn't about to make the same mistake twice, no matter how tempting it might be. Looking back on past encounters, she now realized that Brady deliberately made these outrageous statements to throw her off balance. This time it wouldn't work.

Determined not to rise to the bait, she studiously concentrated on his hands. So Brady was a southpaw, one of those unusually creative people who did things their own way. It figured; he conformed to no one's rules but his own. While he might be infuriating and stubborn, Brady was also trustworthy, an old-fashioned word but applicable all the same.

"You're staring," Brady scolded.

"I'm sorry," she automatically apologized.

"I'll forgive you if you'll go out with me tonight."

Amanda lifted her gaze to the twinkling gleam in his eyes. "Are you sure you want to risk it?" she teased, abandoning her defensive pose and entering into the fray.

His grin widened. "I like living dangerously!"

The words were spoken lightly, but Amanda took them seriously. "Being a cop is already dangerous."

"So's working in a library with a pyromaniac on the loose!" he retorted. "Which reminds me, don't get any ideas about doing a little investigating on your own."

Amanda was startled by his discerning astuteness. How had he known what she'd been thinking? The idea had only just occurred to her anyway. "Why not?" she countered.

"Because this isn't a case for Nancy Drew." Seeing the anger breaking in her eyes, he said quietly but resolutely, "I'm serious, Amanda. You let me do my work and I'll let you get back to yours." He strode across the room, tossing "I'll pick you up at six" over his shoulder as he opened the door.

"Hey, wait a minute!" She grabbed his arm to delay his departure. The muscles of his arm felt like warm steel beneath her fingers. Having successfully stopped him, she quickly released him. "I might have other plans for tonight."

"Do you?"

Something in the directness of his gaze made her admit, "No." Bob had wanted to take her out, after all, it was Friday night, but she'd turned him down, suddenly restless with his staid personality.

"Then I'll pick you up at six," Brady repeated with an intimate smile.

Her mutter of exasperation followed him down the hallway.

Amanda was deliberately slow in preparing for their evening out. It would serve Brady right if he had to wait for her. She wasn't about to bow to his bidding, to rearrange her schedule for his convenience. She handily ignored the fact that she hadn't had anything else planned for the evening, and padded on wet, bare feet from the bathroom to her bedroom closet. It was only when she opened the pair of French doors that she realized she had no idea where Brady planned on taking her tonight, and consequently didn't have a clue of what to wear.

"Damn," she muttered in irritation, impatiently sliding hangers along the metal rod, searching in vain for a perfect outfit, one that would be ideal for any situation. Glancing at the time displayed on her digital alarm clock, she realized that she'd have to find something quickly or else risk having to greet Brady in her present attire of a skimpy towel. It was almost six now.

Since she went on to snag her last pair of panty hose, slacks became the only alternative. She didn't own many pair; most of her wardrobe consisted of interchangeable skirts and jackets. By the time the doorbell rang at a quarter after six, she was still vacillating over what to wear. None of the pants she'd tried on looked right. The black cords she had on now were much tighter than she remembered, definitely not a suitable choice even though they did complement the salmon silk shirt she'd already decided on. The doorbell pealed again, helped along no doubt by an impatient finger held in place.

Amanda opened the door to find Brady leaning on the doorbell. He still wore the same clothes he'd had on when he'd questioned her several hours before.

"Sorry I'm late," he apologized, obviously anticipating her wrath. "Something came up at headquarters."

Her distracted "That's okay" was quickly followed by his murmured "Well, well, well," complete with raised eyebrows.

Immediately on the defensive, Amanda said,

"They're just pants."

Brady's warm gaze rose to her eyes. "Oh, I wasn't looking at the pants. I was admiring what's in them!"

Don't you dare blush, she fiercely instructed herself, cursing the heat she could feel stealing into her cheeks. In an attempt to distract his discerning attention, Amanda directed Brady toward the living room. "Come on in and pour yourself a drink while I finish getting dressed."

"Wait a minute," he instructed, putting his hand on her arm as she had done to him earlier in the day. "Why do you have to change?"

"I can't go out like this," she protested.

"Why not? You look great! So good, in fact, that you might cause a riot. But never fear, I'll be there to protect you!" His voice resumed its teasing inflection.

"You never said where we're going."

"It's a surprise. Come on, let's go." He bundled her into her coat and hustled her out of the house.

"But where are we going?" Amanda repeated as he started the car and pulled out of the drive.

"All right, I'll give you a clue. We're going to see Tempest."

"Shakespeare?" Amanda was disappointed. She didn't feel like sitting through a play tonight, she was too keyed up.

Brady flashed her an affectionately reproving glance as he chided, "No more hints, Mandy."

To Amanda's surprise, they didn't end up in

some experimental playhouse, but in a computerized video game arcade. Dozens of different electronic fantasies stood along the walls, ready to pit their microchip wits against all contenders. Chromatic displays flashed across darkened screens while simulated sound effects of exploding warheads clashed with the futuristic roar of hyperspace. Added to this was the blaring music from a juke box, its overblown speakers distorting what turned out to be an Eagles' song.

The place was crowded, with lines in front of some machines. Amanda had never been inside one of these arcades before and was astonished at how involved the players became. Some were perched on stools, their eyes glued to the artificial world displayed before them. Others were actually dodging the attacking starships, their bodies jerking from side to side.

Brady grasped her hand as a group of teenagers threatened to separate them. Amanda accepted his clasp with appreciation — she didn't relish getting lost in this place. Catching sight of a free machine, Brady tugged her over to it. There, displayed in garish artwork, was the word TEMPEST.

She cracked up. "You've got to be kidding!"

"Hey, I promised you Tempest, didn't I? Never let it be said that Brady Gallagher welched on a promise."

Amanda eyed the unit with amused caution. "I wouldn't know how to begin."

"I'll show you. Here." Brady reached into his

jeans pocket and withdrew a couple of quarters, disproving Amanda's earlier claim that nothing could fit in those tight confines.

A moment later there was a virtual explosion of activity on the screen, as primary-colored spikes and pinwheels threatened destruction. One of them eventually zapped Brady right out of the game.

"Okay. Now it's your turn." He slid another quarter into the slot and placed her hand on the spinning directional wheel.

Amanda gave it her best effort. "Now what's happening?" she exclaimed as the screen first shrank and then expanded.

"You're going on to the next level."

"But I'm not ready yet!" she panicked.

"Sure you are. Keep firing." Brady pressed her finger to the Shoot button. "Watch out! Avoid those spikes!"

Amanda twirled the steering dial. "I'm trying to!"

Five minutes later she turned to him, flushed with victory. "Pretty good, huh?"

"Are you sure you haven't been here before?" he questioned suspiciously, eyeing her outstanding score in disbelief.

"Positive." She grinned at him.

Brady smiled in return, a measure of masculine respect stirred into the warm brown of his eyes. Moving on, they wandered from world to world — dungeons to dragons, explosive missiles to gobbling amoebas.

"You hungry?" Brady asked after Amanda raked up yet another five-digit score.

"Ravenous!"

"Good, because I know a place that serves the best hot dogs you've ever tasted. Hot, juicy, and loaded with sauerkraut."

"Don't say any more," Amanda groaned. "Just lead me to it."

The establishment was small, lending it what Brady laughingly called an intimate atmosphere. They were lucky enough to commandeer one of the four tables the place boasted. Amanda was surprised, but touched, when Brady pulled out a utilitarian chair for her. The chivalrous gesture added yet another dimension to his exasperating, intriguing character.

Brady left Amanda there to stake a claim while he went to place their orders. He returned several minutes later with a tray full of food. The smell of crispy french fries and beefy hot dogs tickled her nose and intrigued her stomach. Even though it was almost nine at night, the place was still alive with people.

Her hot dog was so loaded with goodies that Amanda could hardly fit it into her mouth. As it was, a smudge of mustard dotted her chin. Brady took it upon himself to supervise the cleanup operation, affectionately dabbing her face with a paper napkin.

"There, as good as new," he announced.

"Until the next bite." Amanda grinned before adding, "This really is delicious."

"Of course. The secret is in the authentic sauerkraut."

"And how do you know this is authentic sauerkraut?" she asked, stealing one of his french fries.

Brady watched her munching the stolen plunder with indulgent amusement. "Because I was stationed in Germany when I did my two-year stint in the army."

"Did you enjoy it?"

"The army? Not particularly."

"No, I meant Germany."

"Very much."

"Where exactly were you stationed?"

"In Garmisch."

"That's in the mountains, isn't it?"

"Sure is. Have you ever been there?"

"No. I've always wanted to go to Europe though, especially the Alps."

"I remember seeing that poster of the Alps you've got hanging in your office," Brady acknowledged. "Why haven't you gone?"

Amanda wiped her mouth after downing her last bite of hot dog. "I don't speak the language for one thing."

"Maybe I should offer my services."

"Services?" she repeated suspiciously.

"As a translator, of course," he clarified.

Amanda was impressed. "You speak German?"

"Do I speak German? Does Milwaukee make beer?"

"I gather that's an affirmative," Amanda mocked, pausing to admire the way the corners of his eyes and lips creased simultaneously when he smiled.

"Ten-four," he drawled.

"Is that why you chose to be stationed in Germany? Because you spoke German?"

Brady shook his head. "I didn't know any German before I was stationed there. I took an introductory course on base and then picked up the rest. That's the most natural way to learn a foreign language, through practical usage."

Amanda got the impression that Brady was stating his opinion on all types of learning, that he'd rather go out there and do it, not talk about it in the controlled sterility of a classroom.

"Don't you speak any foreign languages?" he asked, interrupting her silent speculations.

"I had two years of French in college."

"And?" he prompted her.

Amanda's smile was tinged with self-mockery. "And as a result I can ask you, 'Où sont les pommes frites?' "

"It's amazing you learned that much after only two years!" he marveled.

"I've never been good at languages." She shrugged.

Brady's voice lowered intimately, his look one of undivided interest. "What are you good at?"

"Dodging questions like that one," she archly countered, pleased with the way she'd extricated herself. "Did you want that pickle?"

"No, I want to take you to the Oktoberfest."

"In Munich?" Amanda squeaked.

Brady ruefully shook his head. "Not on my salary, no. But with careful planning I might just be able to swing a visit up to Milwaukee's version of Oktoberfest. How about it?"

Amanda had enjoyed their evening together, but it was an enjoyment tinged with an element of danger, for Brady Gallagher had nothing in common with her. He was a streetwise, experienced policeman, while she'd been nurtured in the comparatively sheltered world of academe. But that didn't stop her from wanting to see him, to be with him. Surely she was mature enough to handle her own emotions without letting them get out of hand. They were having an enjoyable, lighthearted relationship, nothing heavy.

"I had no idea that my invitation to spend a day in Milwaukee would require such thought," Brady teased. "A night in Milwaukee, maybe, but not just a day." Amanda's reproving look bounced right off him, like water off a duck's back. "Did you know that your nose sort of scrunches up when you're disapproving?"

Not sure that she liked the sound of a scrunched-up nose, Amanda smoothed out her expression immediately. "It does?"

"Yes. Very cute."

"Cute?"

"Of course. I haven't reached the ripe old age of twenty-eight without learning to recognize a cute nose when I see one."

Amanda almost choked on her pickle. "You're twenty-eight?"

"That's right. Why? How old are you?" he asked with easy familiarity.

Amanda was disgusted to admit that for one fleeting moment she was actually tempted to lie about her age. What had happened to her? How could she even consider altering the truth for vanity's sake?

"I'm old enough to know better," she muttered under her breath, not realizing that Brady could hear her.

He was astonished at her anger. "What's wrong? Are you sensitive about your age?"

"No, I am not sensitive!" she practically shouted. "I'm thirty."

"Well, don't sound so tragic about it."

Amanda wasn't tragic about it; she'd accepted the arrival of her thirtieth birthday without the attendant trauma some people experienced. Having been told even as a teenager that she was "mature for her age," Amanda had always dated men at least four years her senior. Consequently in her own mind there was a world of difference between her age and Brady's.

"Mandy!"

"You can't call a thirty-year-old woman Mandy," she sniped.

"There's no law against it."

"There ought to be," was her muttered response.

"Why? Because it doesn't go with your cool librarian image?"

Amanda was immediately on the defensive.

"It's not an image."

"I think it is. I think that underneath the layers of formality is a little girl who never got the chance to play."

"You're entitled to your opinion, Detective Gallagher."

"How kind, Ms. Richards," he drawled. "Frankly I don't see what you're getting so het up about. There's only two years difference, not twenty!"

"Are you insinuating that I'm old?" she huffily demanded.

"No." Brady leaned across the table. "I'm insinuating that you're young!"

"I'd rather not talk about it."

"I'm sure you wouldn't. That would be very tidy, wouldn't it? Sweeping all your emotions under the carpet like unwanted dust."

Amanda astonished him by laughing. "I do not sweep unwanted dust under the carpet. I use a vacuum cleaner!"

Brady grinned in response to her unexpected flash of humor. "See, it's not so hard to do, is it?"

"What's not so hard?"

"Letting go a little."

"Don't try that inhibited-librarian line on me again, Brady," she warned. "It only worked once."

"And with you once is not enough!"

Coming from any other man, the sexual overtones of the comment would have left her cold, but with Brady there was a spice of wicked excitement that quickened her heart. What was she doing here, sharing provocative retorts in what amounted to little more than an enclosed hot dog stand with a guy who was only in his twenties?

What really bothers you? she asked herself. *Are you having a bad time, or are you worrying about what people might think?* Was Brady right? Was she too wrapped up with her thirty-year-old image to enjoy life? Was it wrong to be aware of your position in life and the responsibilities that it entailed?

Amanda's self-inquisition did not go unnoticed. Brady studied her with an intentness that she would have found discomfiting, had she been aware of it. Brady's hooded eyes roved over her in silent contemplation before he reached out to gently tap her cheek with his lean finger. "Is anyone home in there?" he questioned.

Amanda covered her indecision with an offhand observation. "That's a long trip."

"Not as far as Munich."

"True." Amanda deliberated a moment longer. She'd always wanted to visit Milwaukee's festival, so why not accept? After all, she wasn't agreeing to anything long-term, just a day's outing. "All right. I'd like to go."

"Fine. How about Sunday."

"This Sunday? But that's the day after tomorrow."

"It sure is. Why? Did you have something else planned?"

"I was going to vacuum," Amanda quipped. This lighthearted teasing was, surprisingly, fun. Brady made a tempting verbal sparring partner, and their parity made her wonder how good a partner he'd be in other, more intimate, enterprises. Her body warmed to the thought. This heady enjoyment had never been present with other men she'd dated in the past. Of course she'd never ended the evening licking sauerkraut from her chin either!

Brady returned her banter. "I wouldn't want you rearranging your vacuuming schedule just for me."

"Not for you," Amanda corrected. "For the Oktoberfest."

"You're relegating me to a mere chauffeur, is that it?" he growled.

"If you're good, I might also let you be the tour guide," she offered with mocking generosity.

"Oh, I'm good all right, Mandy," Brady returned, his smile reflecting his wicked amusement. He was feeling quite satisfied with the way things were turning out. Tonight had been a test of sorts, like the one Amanda had subjected him to by taking him to that classical concert. It was a test she'd passed with flying colors, adjusting to the new situation much better than he'd expected.

Sitting across from him, her face animated with amusement, her manner relaxed, Amanda fit in well with her surroundings while still retaining that air of class that had first attracted him to her. The slight difference in their ages was a matter of complete indifference to him. Frankly he was more concerned about the differences in their backgrounds.

Noticing the way her pink tongue was still hungrily licking her lips, Brady offered, "Would you like to sample their Italian ice before we leave?"

"Yes, please," she readily agreed.

The fresh citrus tanginess was a welcome antidote to the aftertaste left by the sauerkraut. Their palates and plates both clean, they dumped their trash in a huge bin, replacing the plastic tray on the shelf reserved for that purpose. The trip back to her house seemed to take less time than the trip out, but maybe that was because now the ice had been broken, and they had temporarily suspended testing! Whatever the reason, Amanda didn't want the evening to end, so she extended it by inviting Brady in for a drink.

"Can I use your phone first?" he asked.

"Sure. It's on the table there." She pointed to the spindle-legged piece of furniture occupying the otherwise unusable space beside the stairs. "What would you like to drink?"

He paused before dialing. "Do you have any beer?"

"I'll go check."

By the time Amanda returned from the kitchen, Brady had completed his phone call and was hanging up the receiver. His sidelong glance encompassed the can of soda in her hand.

"I don't have any beer." Her comment was

in reply to the enquiring tilt of his eyebrow.

Amanda continued on into the living room, followed more closely than she realized by Brady. Turning to offer him the can of carbonated beverage, she was startled by his proximity. His eyes never strayed from hers as he removed the can from her hand, reaching around her to carefully set it on the end table.

"We've been playing games all evening," he murmured, curving his strong hands around the tips of her shoulders and luring her closer.

Amanda avoided the suggestively intimate quality of his low-toned remark. "Of course we've been playing games — Tempest, Pac-Man, Space Invaders . . ."

"That's not what I'm talking about and you know it."

His approach was slow and unthreatening. During those few moments Amanda had ample opportunity to voice her objections. Oddly enough, the words wouldn't come to mind. Instead, her thoughts were flooded with the remembered pleasure of his touch.

Waves of delicious anticipation danced over her as his hands slid across her shoulders. He was so close that the warmth of his breath caressed her sensitive skin. Brady didn't say a word, he didn't have to. The warm desire in his eyes said it all. He deliberately allowed several more emotion-charged seconds to elapse before weaving his fingers into the golden mass of her hair, framing her head with his palms.

Amanda saw his desending mouth through the screen of her downcast lashes. The pressure of his kiss was sensuously light as he explored the possibilities of the caress. Their lips might have been fashioned for each other, so well did they mesh together. There was no bumping of noses, grinding of chins, or clashing of teeth. Tiny, nibbling kisses, tender in nature and devastating in intensity, were bestowed all along the curve of her upper lip. Brady's slow and extended interplay created a momentum of its own.

Amanda's lips parted, her senses filled with the taste of him. Sighing with pleasure, she curved her arms around his neck, her fingers free to roam in the springy curls of his dark hair. As once before, she silently marveled at the ease with which her body fit into his. Her softness melted against his hardness, firing the mounting need pulsing through her blood.

Brady's rising need was apparent as he groaned and gathered her closer. Amanda could feel every muscle and sinew of his masculine frame, taut and unmistakably aroused. His right hand was still entangled in the spun silk of her hair, while the other hand was spread across the small of her back, fusing their lower torsos together in a juncture of erotic stimulation.

Warning bells soon began sounding in Amanda's head, alerting her to the dwindling remnants of her control. Their ringing became increasingly louder, the shrill summons incredibly lifelike. When Brady loosened his embrace, she wondered if he'd heard them too.

He leaned away to lazily study the flushed planes of her face, the glazed bemusement of her eyes. His voice was still husky with desire as he suggested, "I think you'd better answer the phone."

Amanda jerked away from him to do so, reality crowding in on the enticing sensations of a moment ago. "Hello?"

"Is Brady Gallagher there?" a feminine voice inquired.

"Yes, he is. Just a minute, please." Amanda put her hand over the mouthpiece and held out the receiver. "It's for you," she told Brady.

Amanda could ascertain nothing from Brady's monosyllabic responses into the phone. The conversation was brief, and judging by the look on his face, serious.

"What's wrong?" she asked as soon as he hung up.

His reply made her stomach plummet. "There's been another fire at the college."

Chapter Four

Brady had already pulled on his vest by the time Amanda found her voice. “How bad is it? Was anyone hurt?”

Brady answered her last question first. “No, no one was hurt. It was a small fire, in a trash can in a washroom on the third floor. The college security people caught it before it had time to spread. Listen, I’ve got to go. I’ll talk to you later.”

He let himself out, a concerned Amanda remaining behind. There was no doubt that the situation was a potentially dangerous one. Had the fire spread, there could have been numerous injuries, even fatalities. What kind of maniac would endanger the lives of hundreds of people in such a way? Who could be setting these fires, and why?

Assuming that their intended jaunt to the Oktoberfest in Milwaukee would be postponed until another time, Amanda didn’t expect to hear from Brady again that weekend. Consequently she was surprised when he called late Saturday night. She’d just returned from a date with Bob, and was mentally kicking herself for accepting his invitation. It had not been an enjoyable evening. She no longer found Bob to be the least bit stimulating, either mentally or physically. In fact, he was decidedly dull!

The phone was ringing as she let herself into the otherwise quiet house. In her hurry to answer it, Amanda tripped over the phone's extension cord, pulling the entire unit onto the floor. The resultant crash did put a stop to the ringing because the receiver skidded across the hardwood floor. Amanda scrambled after it. "Hello?"

"Mandy, are you all right?" a male voice urgently questioned.

"Brady?"

"Yes, it's Brady. Answer me! Are you all right?"

"Of course I'm all right," she retorted impatiently, resenting his tone. "Why wouldn't I be?"

"Because it sounded as though you were wrestling for the telephone!"

"Not *for* the phone, *with* the phone. It fell on the floor."

"Did you lock your front door?" he confused her by asking.

"Lock . . . I don't know. What's that got to do with anything?"

"Mandy, you're living there alone, and it would be advisable for you to keep the door locked at night."

"Yes, Detective Gallagher. Thank you so much for the safety lecture. Was that all?"

"No, that's not all. Be ready at eight in the morning."

"Ready for what?"

"Me. I'm taking you to the Oktoberfest in Milwaukee, or had you forgotten?"

"No, I didn't forget," she answered. "I just thought that with the second fire at the college you might not be able to get away this weekend."

"I'm not getting away for the weekend," he replied. "Only for the day. And I've earned a break. I've been working since early this morning."

"Then maybe you should take it easy tomorrow. After all, Sunday is supposed to be a day of rest."

"You're not getting out of it that easily," he warned her.

"I'm not trying to get out of anything, Brady. I just thought you might be tired."

"Then maybe you should let me go get some sleep so I can pick you up in the morning. Good night, Mandy. See you at eight."

He hung up before she could say a word. Amanda slammed the receiver back on its cradle, rattling the bell inside the central mechanism.

Had it not meant getting up even earlier the next morning, she would have been sorely tempted to leave before Brady's arrival. He had no right to play the domineering drill sergeant with her! Muttering under her breath about the foibles of the male half of the human race, she returned the phone to the table before checking to make sure the front door was locked. The safety check had been part of her nightly ritual since her first apartment, and inherent to her cautious nature.

So why did Brady treat her like a half-wit, accusing her of not knowing left from right, of being unable to automatically lock the doors at night? *Stop being so touchy,* her practical side advised. *Go to bed. Tomorrow's going to be a long day and you're going to need a clear head.*

Of course getting a good night's rest is sometimes easier said than done. By six forty-five the next morning, Amanda had already been checking the time at five-minute intervals for the last half hour.

"This is ridiculous," she muttered, kicking aside her Dacron-filled comforter.

She padded across the hall into the bathroom and stood under a refreshing shower. The massaging spray soothed the remaining tension from her neck and upper back. Exactly thirty-six minutes later she was downstairs and fully-dressed. After some initial hesitation she'd decided on a pair of beige chinos and a blue oxford-cloth shirt. The overall effect was a tailored casualness that she found pleasing. Whether Brady found it so, or not, was his problem!

Brady rang the front doorbell just as she was rinsing out her coffee cup and cereal bowl in the kitchen. Even from the hallway, the top of his dark, curly hair was visible through the portal's diamond-shaped window. Taking a deep breath, she willed her uneven heartbeat to steady itself before opening the door.

"Good morning, Mandy." He greeted her with that special smile of his. "Are you ready to go?"

"Just about," she replied.

"Well, hurry it up!"

"What's the rush?"

"I've got a surprise for you!"

"I don't know if I can handle another one."

"What are you muttering about? I haven't given you any surprises yet."

"Really? What about taking me to the arcade on Friday?"

Brady hooked his thumbs around the belt loops of his jeans, resting his hands on his lean hips in an attitude of relaxed assurance. "I gave you a hint."

"That's right, Tempest, knowing I'd assume it was the play by Shakespeare."

"Did Shakespeare write a play called Tempest?" he questioned with feigned ignorance, his eyes sparkling with impish humor.

"Don't play dumb, Brady. You knew that's what I'd think."

"Just like you knew I'd think we were going to a popular concert that first night."

"Classical music is popular," Amanda retorted.

"You know what I mean."

She couldn't deny it. "If I surprised you, then you got even on Friday night. Can't we call it quits?"

"Do I look like a quitter?"

"You didn't play Tempest like a quitter," she

had to admit with a smile.

"Neither did you," he countered. "I had no idea librarians were so competitive!"

"Are you still upset because I beat you?"

"That was beginner's luck," he dismissed.

"You're asking for it," Amanda warned, shaking her finger at him.

"I know," Brady intimately acknowledged. "But you haven't given it to me yet!"

How could she begin to describe those looks he gave her? They consisted of equal parts of deliberate suggestiveness, sexual awareness, and latent desire. It made for a potent combination! And when the play of words was added to the skirmish, Amanda was hard pressed to maintain her distance.

"I thought you were in a hurry to go," she countered, gathering up her sweater and purse.

"I am." Brady took her wrap away and held it up invitingly. Amanda slid her arms in, but the knit material of the sweater got caught on the cotton of her oxford shirt. Her face grew warm from her struggles.

"Stop fighting it." Brady's suggestion was murmured in her ear, stirring the golden strands of her hair and agitating her even more.

"Fighting what?" Was that breathless voice really hers?

"Your sweater. What else?"

What else indeed? she thought to herself.

Brady turned Amanda around to face him. "You look great!"

"I wasn't sure what to wear," she found herself admitting.

"I can't imagine your not being sure of anything." His teasing inflection disguised the fact that he was half serious. "Let's go."

Amanda's first surprise turned out to be the vintage Mustang parked in the driveway. Despite its age, it was in excellent condition. "Is this yours?"

"No," Brady mocked. "I stole it."

"Ask a silly question," she paraphrased under her breath.

"Talking to yourself again, Mandy? That's a sure sign that you need a break."

Amanda couldn't resist a smile of anticipation as Brady shunned the expressway in favor of picturesque country roads. Located equidistant between the Mississippi River and Lake Michigan, Deerfield was surrounded by lush and rolling farmland. Their route twisted over ridges and dipped past hollows adorned with brilliant sugar maples and russet oaks. Entire hillsides were ablaze with color — brilliant yellows, golds, and reds, with just enough evergreens for contrast.

"What are you smiling at?" Brady asked.

"It's funny how some people think of Wisconsin as a level cow pasture."

Brady flicked a glance at the passing landscape. "Amazing what a few glaciers can do!"

Brady's scheduled surprise turned out to be a stop at a roadside stand displaying baskets of ruby, gold, and green apples. Trees laden with fruit lined both sides of the road. The air was rich with the type of crisp, butter-colored sunlight that was indigenous to fall.

"How do you fancy a toffee apple for a mid-morning snack?" he asked.

Bob would have been horrified had he seen the eagerness with which Amanda accepted. He would never have been caught dead munching on such a sticky childhood delight. But the farther away they got from Deerfield, the more relaxed Amanda became. She forgot how she was supposed to act and simply enjoyed herself. She and Brady settled on a picnic table facing the orchard, enjoying the beautiful day and their treat. The sweet, chewy caramel and the crisp, tart fruit created a flavor that was hard to beat.

"Are you sure you're not too tired to drive all the way to Milwaukee?" Amanda worried. "You had a long day yesterday, maybe you should've stayed in bed."

"Is that an offer?"

"Brady, I'm serious!"

"I can tell you are. Your forehead is pleated."

"Pleated?"

"Mmm. Like this." He frowned ferociously.

"Thanks," Amanda muttered, suddenly losing her appetite. First he told her she had a scrunched-up nose and now a pleated forehead. Great! All she needed was a seam around her throat and she could apply to be the bride of Frankenstein.

"I was only kidding. Can't you take a joke?"

Amanda gave him a dose of his own medicine. "It was obvious that you were kidding, your eyes were creased!"

Brady grinned appreciatively. "I like it when you tease me back, Mandy."

"You do, do you?"

"Mmm." He reached out a finger to wipe away the trickle of apple juice that moistened her lips. "I also like the way you kiss."

Brady jerked his finger back as it was almost included with her next bite of toffee apple. "Hey!"

"Don't you know that it's dangerous to get between a woman and her apple?" she mocked.

"No, but I'm learning."

"Funny, I would've said you were a *fast* learner," Amanda mused.

"Depends on the topic," Brady countered. "Certain subjects deserve more intense study." His eloquent gaze made it clear that he considered her such a subject.

"Did you always want to be a policeman?" Amanda asked once they were back on the road. She recognized a kindred inner determination that told her Brady could have been anything he'd wanted, and she was curious about his motivations for staying in Deerfield.

"No." He reached for a pair of sunglasses hanging from the rearview mirror and slid them on before continuing. "When I was a kid I wanted to be an accountant."

Amanda cracked up. "Really?"

"What do you think?" he tossed back.

"That you've probably always wanted to be a cop."

"I suppose that might explain why I set up a detective agency in the back of the garage."

Amanda didn't notice at the time, but Brady had adroitly succeeded in appearing to answer her question without actually doing so. "You had your own detective agency?"

"Sure did. I must've fingerprinted everyone on the block, at least those I could get my hands on."

"What happened then?"

"When I got my hands on them?"

"No, what happened to the detective agency?"

"My sister appropriated it when I entered high school and I discovered more stimulating things to do with my hands."

"I can imagine," she remarked dryly.

"Can you really?" Brady reached out to place a warm hand on the curve of her knee. "Why don't you tell me about it?" he invited.

"Because I'd rather you kept your mind on your driving and your hands on the wheel." She lifted his hand and returned it to the steering column.

Several hours, four beers, three bratwurst, and two hot pretzels later, they stood on Milwaukee's lakeshore, admiring the view.

"Thanks for bringing me." Amanda's voice drifted up from Brady's shoulder, where she was resting her head. It was suddenly impressed upon her how compatable his height was with her's.

The placement of his shoulder was perfect for laying her head on, without having to crane her neck or stand on tiptoe. With a happy sigh she settled herself more comfortably against him and murmured, "I really had a good time."

"I'm glad." His voice warmed her inside.

"Did your beer taste as good as mine?" She lifted her head to question Brady with wonder. Her dark eyes reflected the lights along the lake as she stared up at him, raptly awaiting his reply.

Having never been subjected to the full force of her undivided attention, and already feeling besieged by her cuddly body, Brady had to clear his throat before agreeing. "The beer was great." He was beginning to have his doubts about the advisability of allowing her to drink those last two steins. Mandy was hard enough to handle when she was sober, she could be irresistible when tipsy.

"I loved the folk dancers," she dreamily continued as they turned and strolled back to the car. "And the brass bands. Do you remember the tuba player in that first band?"

Brady had to laugh at Amanda's impersonation, puffed-out cheeks and all! She was adorable, but definitely tipsy.

They didn't get back to Deerfield until after midnight. Luckily for Brady's peace of mind, when Amanda fell asleep on the way home she snuggled against the vinyl upholstery instead of him. His thoughts were chaotic enough as it was. He couldn't remember a day he'd enjoyed more.

Today he'd seen another side of Amanda, a carefree side that he found captivating.

When Brady brought the Mustang to a smooth stop in front of Amanda's house, his hand reached out to gently shake her shoulder. "Mandy?"

Her lids drowsily rose, and the darkened pools of her eyes blinked at him owlishly.

"We're home," he explained.

"Did I fall asleep?"

"Yep. Come on, princess, before this coach turns into a pumpkin."

"What time is it?" she questioned bemusedly as he guided her to the front door.

"After midnight." Brady watched her fumble with the key before instructing her. "Here, you'd better let me do that."

Once the door was unlocked, he pushed it open and ushered her in. Amanda thought she gracefully floated across the threshold, but in reality she tripped over it and nearly stumbled.

"Careful," Brady cautioned, gripping her shoulders from behind to prevent her from landing flat on her face.

"I'm always careful," she loftily informed him.

"Usually," he ruefully amended.

Amanda stifled a yawn. "If I weren't so tired, I'd be tempted to ask what you meant by that."

If she weren't so tired and not quite responsible for her actions, Brady would have been tempted to do a lot more than just ask questions!

Amanda had no idea of the direction of Brady's thoughts, engrossed as she was in trying to undo the wooden buttons of her sweater. Her normally dexterous fingers had become all thumbs as they struggled with the fastenings. With an exasperated sigh, Brady gently shoved her hands out of the way and unworked the buttons himself.

Amanda looked up, expecting him to be concentrating on his self-appointed task. Instead, she discovered his gaze was fixed on her parted mouth, studying it with incredible hunger. Amanda closed her eyes in order to shut out the disturbing image, but that only made matters worse. Now her senses were free to concentrate on the evocative touch of his hands. Their progressive descent was marked by a whisper-soft passage against the curve of her breasts, the planes of her stomach, until the very last button was undone.

Not a word passed between them; this wasn't the time to verbalize, it was a time for sensual communication. Her eyes flickered open as Brady brushed her cheek with the back of his knuckles. One lean index finger trailed down the curve of her face, pausing to trace a series of intricate spirals at the base of her jawline.

Their eyes were inexorably interwoven, Amanda's holding an element of confusion while Brady's were warm with desire. His thumb swung to the corner of her mouth and back again, the oscillating caress making her long for his kiss. But it never came.

Brady's husky "Good night" had barely registered in her ears before he was gone, closing the front door behind him. Amanda stood where he'd left her, gazing in disbelief at the solid wood panels. He'd left without kissing her! Brady had awakened a Pandora's box of desire in her otherwise sleepy body, only to walk out on the dénouement. Too tired to unravel the events of the day, Amanda locked the door and got ready for bed. She fell asleep as soon as her head hit the pillow, her dreams picking up where Brady had left off!

Monday morning the main topic of conversation at work was still the weekend's pyromaniacal display. In their excitement about the latest fire, her coworkers were slow to notice Amanda's air of dreamy preoccupation. It wasn't until Helen asked how her weekend went that Amanda came to life.

"It was great!" she exclaimed, repeating Brady's favorite adjective. "I went to Milwaukee on Sunday, to the Oktoberfest. Have you ever gone?"

Helen shook her head.

"You really should! It's patterned after the old-world festival in Munich. We had a wonderful time! There were groups of folk dancers and German brass bands. The place was full of color and life with lots of traditional *Gemütlichkeit.* The food was fabulous and . . ."

She paused at the look of amusement on Helen's face. "It was very nice," Amanda concluded with more customary decorum.

Beth and Helen had to grin at each other across the room after Amanda left for a library faculty committee meeting.

"Her trip to the Oktoberfest must have really been something," Helen mused. "Amanda isn't usually so effervescent!"

"I know. I imagine the company had something to do with it," was Beth's hunch.

"You mean Brady Gallagher?" Helen turned to ask her.

"Well, I can't see Bob taking her to Milwaukee for a beer festival!"

"I think they're a cute couple," Helen benevolently decreed.

"Amanda and Bob?" Beth questioned in a horrified fashion.

"No," Helen corrected. "Amanda and Brady."

"You've got that matchmaking gleam in your eye again, Helen."

The older woman tossed her head. "Nonsense. I was just stating an opinion, that's all."

Amanda's meeting ran late. John was playing head honcho by expounding on his master plan for the library's grandiose future, wasting time that should have been used to discuss the current problems that needed immediate attention. Guy Lox had been obnoxious as usual, his petulant voice grating on Amanda's nerves. She was nursing a full-blown headache by the time she returned to the comparative haven of her own office. Beth knocked on the adjoining door a few moments later.

"How did the meeting go?"

"I'll give you one guess," Amanda returned,

pulling a bottle of aspirin out of her desk's top drawer.

"Don't tell me . . ."

"I'm trying not to," Amanda assured her with a grimace.

"How about lunch?" Beth asked, interrupting Amanda's muttered commentary about Guy Lox's lineage.

"I'm too angry to eat!"

"Then I'll tell you something that will cheer you up." Beth paused a moment in order to build the suspense. "Brady stopped in to see you."

Amanda bristled. "And why should that cheer me up?"

"You're not still denying it, are you?"

"I don't have the faintest idea what you're talking about," Amanda loftily returned.

"Don't tell me you're still pretending not to be interested in Brady."

"I'm not pretending anything," Amanda denied. "Brady and I are friends, nothing more. What did he want?"

"He didn't say. He did look tired though."

"We didn't get in until late last night," Amanda absently explained, studying a memo from the dean that she'd just found on top of her desk. Beth's continued silence finally caused her to look up. The foregone conclusion written on her friend's face made Amanda voice a reprimanding exclamation. "Beth!"

"I didn't say a word," Beth innocently protested, her blue eyes sparkling.

"You didn't have to."

"I can't help it. I've seen the way Brady looks at you."

"And how do you think he looks at me?" Amanda's voice was studiously nonchalant.

"It isn't something you can put in words," Beth finally said. "It's too elusive for that."

"I'm sure it is," Amanda wryly replied, silently kicking herself for asking in the first place. "Come on, let's go eat."

"But I thought you said you were too angry to be hungry."

"Eating is preferable to being subjected to the third degree."

"If you don't want to talk about it, all you have to do is tell me," Beth retorted with affected huffiness.

"I don't want to talk about it," Amanda promptly stated.

"Fine. I'm not the kind of friend that will hold a grudge against someone just because they clam up."

"Clams! Perfect. How about going to that new seafood restaurant for lunch?"

The suggestion successfully diverted Beth's attention. Their lunch hour passed without further mention of Brady. The aspirin hadn't helped her headache much, just dulled it to a vague annoyance. Walking back to her office with Beth, Amanda was absently rubbing the back of her neck when she got the funny sensation that someone was watching her. She looked up and found

Brady propped against her closed office door, one hand thrust into his jeans pocket. He was obviously waiting for her.

"Hi, Beth. How's the head today, Mandy?"

"My head is fine, thank you," she replied, unlocking her office under his leisurely gaze.

Brady grinned conspiratorially at Beth before asking Amanda, "No aftereffects from all the beer?"

Her expression was one of censorious protest. "You make it sound like I was drunk."

"No, you weren't drunk." He straightened up and followed Amanda and Beth into the office.

"Of course not." Amanda's reply was unknowingly haughty.

"A little high, perhaps."

Beth's stifled laughter was clearly audible across the room, but Amanda was not amused. "Brady!"

His look was one of boyish innocence. "Well, you were."

"I was not."

"Oh, I get it." He nodded knowingly. "Your memory of last night is a little hazy, right?"

"No, that's not right!"

"Don't tell me. It's not right, it's left, right?"

Beth found Brady's last statement incomprehensible and said so. "What are you two talking about?"

Brady obligingly turned to explain. "Your friend here has a little problem telling her left from right."

"I do not," Amanda fiercely denied.

"Then put out your left hand."

Amanda had to pause a moment, and was lost.

"See," Brady teased. "She has to think about it first. Very cautious is our Amanda!"

Beth's appreciative grin was tinged with more than a hint of admiration. She'd never seen anyone treat Amanda with such raillery. No man had ever dared. But courage did not seem to be a trait that Brady Gallagher lacked!

Amanda was very much aware of Beth's amusement and took out her frustration on the cause of her discomfiture — Brady. "Did you come here for a reason? Other than making fun of me, I mean. Because, if not, I do have more important things to do than play games with you."

"I can't imagine what. Okay." Brady put up his hand to forestall her furious response. "I was just kidding, Mandy. Actually I stopped by to ask if you'd seen Guy Lox today."

"Yes, he was at this morning's library committee meeting. Why?"

Brady shrugged, momentarily drawing her attention to the powerful width of his shoulders. "I got a message that he wanted to see me, and his secretary seemed to think that he'd be here in the library."

"I believe he and John went out to lunch. They may not be back until late." This was one of John's favorite ways of avoiding work, the all-afternoon lunch.

"Well, if it's important, Lox will just have to get in touch with me some other time."

"Any leads on the arson case?" Beth inserted.

Brady wearily shook his head. "Nothing concrete. Listen, I've got to get back to headquarters. I'll see you later, Mandy."

But he didn't. In fact, Amanda didn't see him again until Thursday. She knew he'd been terribly busy with the arson investigation, questioning people for a possible lead. The students, who weren't exactly enamored with the police to start off with, were very vocal in their dissatisfaction and Brady had been called upon to speak to them this morning. Amanda had managed to slip away to the auditorium and listen to part of his presentation. He handled himself well, never losing control of the situation. Several students tried to put him on the defensive by attacking his investigation and demanding immediate results. But Brady was accustomed to dealing with more virulent attacks than those provided by the students and withstood the barrage without any difficulty.

Amanda felt a rush of what could almost have been proud affection at the sight of his familiar jeaned figure. Was she the only one present who knew Brady was left-handed, that he liked sauerkraut on his hot dogs, that he enjoyed both classical music and electronic games? *What's that got to do with anything?* her conscience demanded. *Haven't you got better things to do than stand here mooning over a policeman still in his twenties?* The answer was yes, there were any number of things she should have been doing, including keeping an appointment she'd set up with a sales representative from a library supply house. Amanda slipped out of the auditorium, and returned to work.

She encountered Brady in the hallway a few hours later. After the fiasco he'd put her through the last time they'd met in her office, she knew she should display regal disinterest. She really did try to cultivate her anger, but Brady's exhausted appearance foiled her intentions.

"You look tired," she noted.

"I'm okay," Brady murmured. "You sound almost worried about me."

"Maybe I am almost worried about you."

"I saw you in the auditorium this morning. Why'd you leave so early? Was my voice putting you to sleep?"

"I had to get back to work."

"And I suppose I wasn't meant to notice you there in the first place," Brady astutely guessed.

"I didn't say that."

"I know you didn't, but you were sitting in the last row."

"You handled the students very well," Amanda complimented, hoping to divert his attention.

"Handled?" He questioned her use of the word.

She eyed him in exasperation. "You know what I mean."

"Sorry." Tired though he was, his eyes still held a glimmer of devilment. "I can't seem to resist teasing you."

"Why not?"

"Don't know." He shook his head. "Must be

something to do with your blond hair, or maybe it's your big brown eyes."

"Are you sure it isn't my scrunched-up nose or my pleated forehead?" she joked.

"Now that you mention it . . ."

Amanda put up her hands in defeat. "Forget I asked."

"I'd never forget anything you asked, Mandy." Despite the noise of passing students, Brady was still able to inflect a degree of intimacy into the statement, making it sound like a devoted promise.

She stopped fighting. "Would you like to have dinner at my place?"

"Can you cook?"

"You'll have to decide that for yourself."

"There's no time like the present. How about tonight?"

"Tonight, um . . ." She floundered for a moment before agreeing. "Okay, tonight. Seven o'clock," she added before he made it any earlier.

"I'll try and hold off until then."

"I'm sure you can manage it," she affirmed. "Remember your army combat training!"

Amanda didn't have time to both change out of her work clothes and prepare dinner, so she had to make do with removing her suit jacket and opening the top buttons of her plum silk blouse. She put on a bib-type apron to protect her clothing. During the short drive home from work, she had put together a menu in her head. Beef Stroganoff for the main course, with a salad and a frozen vegetable. A quick stop at the local bakery had supplied dessert — a strawberry-rhubarb pie.

The meat was simmering in its own juices when she left the kitchen to set the dining room table. A white tablecloth with a centerpiece of driftwood and ivy was the backdrop for the table settings of space-age, unbreakable dinnerware. Amanda unsuccessfully tried to catch a glimpse of her appearance in the flat surface of the dishes. *I must be using the wrong dishwashing detergent,* she laughed to herself. She decided against using the candlesticks that adorned the sideboard. "This is just a friendly dinner," she explained to them, as if they could hear her.

Back in the kitchen, Amanda placed a package of frozen peas in her space-saving microwave and prepared a tossed salad. The Stroganoff's smooth, golden-brown sauce was near perfection as she poured it into a warming dish. Thank God it hadn't curdled when she'd added the sour cream!

The summons of the doorbell interrupted her prayer of thankfulness. While hurrying to answer it, Amanda was removing her apron with one hand and tidying her hair with the other. This left no time to check the caller's identity by looking through the door's diamond-shaped window. Expecting to find Brady, Amanda was dismayed to discover Bob Mason sedately standing on her front porch.

Chapter Five

Bob, what a surprise!" Amanda exclaimed, surreptitiously checking her watch. She had about five minutes to get rid of Bob before Brady was due to arrive, providing he didn't come early.

"I'm sorry I didn't call first," Bob began.

So am I, she mentally agreed.

". . . but I was in the neighborhood and thought I might as well drop by to ask you about the country club's annual dinner."

Amanda had never noticed before how slowly Bob spoke, drawing out each syllable and pausing between each word. Or did it only seem that way because she was so eager to get rid of him?

"What about the annual dinner?" she pressed, urging him to get to the point.

"Did you want to go with me again this year?"

"But the dinner isn't until Christmas, is it?"

"That's right."

"I'm not sure I can make a commitment that far in advance."

Bob was surprised. "Why, Amanda, this doesn't sound like you at all. Normally you prefer things settled ahead of time."

"Can I check back with you tomorrow, Bob?"

"I suppose so," he reluctantly agreed.

"Fine. I'll call you." Amanda reached for the

door and abruptly pulled it open as a sign of dismissal. Brady, who was preparing to knock on her door, almost rapped on her forehead instead. He quickly lowered his hand, his warm smile of pleasure fading at the sight of Bob standing behind her.

"These are for you." He shoved a bunch of marigolds into her hands. "Sorry I didn't get any for you, Bob, but I didn't think orange was your color."

"What are you doing here, Gallagher?"

Amanda grimaced at the deliberately belligerent tone of Bob's voice.

Surprisingly Brady didn't return the anger, although he did return the question. "I was just about to ask the same of you, Mason."

"I'm here to speak to Amanda."

Sensing that this was the time to call an end to their verbal circling, Amanda intervened. "I think we've pretty well covered everything, Bob. I'll get back to you tomorrow, all right?"

"Fine. I'll look forward to hearing from you." A stiff nod was the only acknowledgment he gave Brady, who stepped aside to let him pass.

"Drop by any time, Mason," Brady invited. "Mandy and I are always happy to see you."

Amanda shut the door before Brady could wave any more red flags.

"Don't expect to get rid of me that easily," he warned her.

"It's encouraging to know that your self-preservation system is warning you that I'd love to get rid of you."

"Is that all you'd love to do to me, Mandy?" His question was accompanied by one of those devilishly naughty looks that he specialized in.

"You're impossible!"

"Totally," he agreed with a grin. "Is dinner ready? I'm starved."

"You may be starved, but I'm not sure you deserve to be fed after that performance."

"You would deny a man in blue his daily meal?" Brady questioned in horror.

"What do you think?"

"I think I'd better be on my best behavior if I want to sample your culinary delights."

"That's better," she approved. "And thank you for the flowers."

"Don't mention it. I stole them from your garden!"

Amanda had to laugh at his ready confession.

The dinner was a great success. Brady helped himself to seconds and thirds, heaping extravagant compliments on Amanda in much the same way that he kept heaping piles of noodles on his dish.

"I hope you like strawberry-rhubarb pie," she said as she placed the dessert on the table.

"You've gotta be kidding! Strawberry-rhubarb is my favorite!"

"Mine too," she confessed, slicing into the fruit-filled pie. Once the dessert was served, Amanda lifted the coffeepot in a gesture of invitation. "Would you like some?"

"Is it decaffeinated?"

"Yes, it is."

"Good. Because with you around, I don't need any additional stimulation."

"What happened to all your combat training?" she countered with an arch glance, no mean feat when done while pouring a cup of coffee.

"I must've missed the class on handling forward librarians."

"Forward! I like that."

"Me too," he grinned.

"I am not forward."

He lifted his brows. "Why not?"

"Drink your coffee before it gets cold."

"Yes, ma'am," he mockingly agreed.

After their meal Brady surprised her by offering to clean up.

"That's all right. I've heard that the kitchen can be a dangerous place for southpaws."

"It's true, but how do you know that?"

"I read it somewhere," she shrugged. There was no way she was going to confess to reading up on southpaws in the hope of discovering what made Brady Gallagher tick!

"One of the dangers of dating a librarian, I suppose."

"Only one of them? What are the rest?"

"Ah, that would be telling. Since you won't allow me to help you with all this, what do you say to leaving it here while we go settle somewhere more comfortable."

"Like the living room?"

"If that's the best you can do." His look suggested that the bedroom would be more appropriate for what he had in mind.

"You've got a one-track mind!" she accused him.

"It's eight-track," he corrected, "and they're all playing the same thing!"

"Are you for real?" she groaned with a laugh.

"Why don't you come over here and find out," he murmured, patting the seat next to him invitingly.

"I might just do that."

"Promises, promises," he sighed. "Which brings me to the next topic of conversation. Didn't I promise to help you overcome this problem you've got with left and right?"

Amanda deliberately chose an armchair across from the couch as she denied, "I don't have any problem."

"Scared?"

"No."

"Then why are you sitting way over there? I don't bite. Unless asked to," he added provocatively.

The communication sent by his slumberous gaze beckoned her closer until she was sitting right beside him. His hand then lifted to push a strand of blond hair away from her face before shifting to trail down the side of her face, his finger finally lazily circling a corner of her mouth. This was one of the things that made Brady's embraces so special. He never simply kissed her. Each kiss was preceded by a caress as he cupped her face, ran his fingers through her hair, or tested the contours of her lower lip with his thumb. Amanda saw his dark head lower to hers before her eyelids dropped, shielding the curious expectation reflected in her bemused eyes. She waited with bated breath for the touch of his lips on hers, but instead she felt the soft whisper of his words.

"This is your left temple." His mouth brushed over the cataloged item, sampling her as though she were a choice delicacy for his consumption. Only when that territory had been completely surveyed did Brady move on, nuzzling aside the silky mass of her hair to expose the delicate curve of her ear. Thrown by the sensual turmoil his tactile caresses were generating, Amanda made no move to stop the erotic inventory. Her system was filled with a paralyzing sweetness that was prolonged by the lingering inspection of his lips.

His voice rippled over her skin as he huskily listed, "Left shoulder."

The warmth of his palm radiated through her, touching the receptiveness of tingling nerve endings. "Left arm."

Amply assisted by the sleek material of her silk blouse, his hand leisurely cruised down the length of her arm. The memory of his touch was retained long after he'd moved on, so that by the time he reached her hand, Amanda's entire arm was alive with a wildfire of excitation. "Left hand."

Brady felt the fine tremors shaking her hand

as he slid his fingers between hers. Lifting her hand to his mouth, he flicked the tip of his tongue across her knuckles in a way that was guaranteed to increase her trembling. Glowing splinters of desire punctuated her composure, leaving her prey to the raw needs prowling through her. Her hand opened to cup his lean cheek, guiding his tempting mouth to the parted sweetness of her lips.

The depth of her response was more than either one of them had expected, and Brady's emotions flared in reply. Expecting him to continue his downward travels, she was surprised when he started all over again, this time starting with her right temple, so that by the time he reached her right hand, it was already spread across his back.

Moments later Amanda found herself draped across Brady's lap, very much aware of the taut contours of his body. It took only a dexterous twist to have them both stretched out full-length on the couch. She didn't have time to contemplate the possible repercussions, because his lips joined in the subtle seduction, and rational thought dimmed accordingly.

His touch was embroidered with intimacy as his hand circled behind her ear to slowly meander down her neck. The throbbing pulse at the base of her throat told its own story, one that Brady paused to relish. "Your heart's pounding," he informed her softly.

Amanda slowly raised her hand to his chest, the thin material of his shirt acting like a second skin. "So's yours," she answered with husky unsteadiness.

Brady's nimble fingers undid the few remaining buttons until her blouse fell open, revealing the shimmering delicacy of her lingerie. Instead of providing protection from his caresses, the thin nylon of her slip turned his touch into a silky temptation, his featherlight stroking movements igniting new flames in the fire of her desire. His slow touch was far more arousing than any impatient fondling, and it put the other embraces she'd experienced to shame.

Amanda slid her arms out of the sleeves of her blouse and lifted them to his shoulders, enjoying the feel of the strong column of his neck rubbing against the bare skin of her inner arm. Drifting closer to him, she clasped her arms tightly around his neck and mindlessly guided his lips back to hers for a kiss of unrestrained passion. His mouth readily assimilated hers, his warm tongue drawing hers into an intimate dialogue. The languid tousle was intensely evocative. She returned his play with hungry fire, arching her body against his.

Their emotions were running high, their self-control low, when the sound of the doorbell invaded their idyllic haven.

Brady's mouth eased slightly to whisper, "Don't answer it. They'll go away."

He was right, they did go away, but the sound of the doorbell was replaced by the clamoring demands of the phone.

With a frustrated groan, Brady pried himself away from her. "Damn! It could be headquarters. We've got to answer it."

Amanda was already rolling off the couch. There didn't seem to be much point in trying to replace her blouse, so she didn't bother. Brady's eyes followed her as she moved across the room, noting her elegant carriage and exquisite body. He also observed the change in her manner the moment she identified the caller. Amanda didn't stay on the phone for long; Brady heard her brief explanation that she had company. But by the time she hung up, her barriers had all been replaced, and the warm, loving woman he'd held in his arms was gone.

"What's wrong?" Brady queried, her abrupt mood reversal throwing him off-balance.

"Nothing." Her voice was cool as she efficiently picked up her blouse and put it back on before walking over to the bar and pouring herself a sherry.

"Talk to me," he coaxed as he walked over to her. His hand on her arm prevented her from turning away.

There was a certain soothing comfort in his touch that got through to her and made her say, "That was my mother. She was calling from California."

"Is something wrong with her?"

"Yes," Amanda flatly replied. "But not in the way you mean. She just got married again."

"Isn't that good news?"

"Not when it's for the fourth time."

Even Brady looked surprised. "She's been married four times?"

Amanda laughed bitterly. "My mother is a staunch supporter of the institution of marriage."

"Come on, Mandy. Let's sit down and talk about it. The news has obviously upset you."

But Amanda was no longer in a receptive mood. "Look, Brady, we've had our fun and games. Now it's time for you to leave."

"Mandy, I warned you that you weren't going to be able to get rid of me as easily as you did that klutzy accountant."

"I'll call the police," she threatened without thinking.

"They already know I'm here," Brady grinned in amusement.

"What do you want?" Her voice was ragged with repressed emotion.

"Ultimately, you. But for the time being I'll settle for a little information. You never talk about your family. Why is that?"

"My family life hasn't been as happy as yours," she countered bitterly.

Brady's expression suddenly became austere. "My family life hasn't always been happy, Mandy. I was twenty-three when we learned that my father had lung cancer. He'd been a heavy smoker, but the ironic thing is that he'd finally quit smoking a couple months earlier."

"I'm sorry." The words seemed inadequate somehow. "I didn't know."

"There are a lot of things about me you don't know, Mandy. Things you don't bother to find out. The reason I don't smoke is just one of them."

"It's not in my nature to delve into other people's personal lives." She defended her attitude.

"Why not? Afraid they might return the favor?"

Amanda wearily shoved her hair away from her face. "Brady, I don't find it easy to talk about my past."

"I realize that," he said in a softer tone. "And I'm not pressing for your life story. I'd just like you to open up a little, Mandy. I want to be your friend."

"Just my friend?"

"And your lover."

"No one could accuse you of beating around the bush," she wryly observed.

"You did ask," he reminded her.

"So? Since when have you started doing what I ask?"

"I like to indulge you occasionally. And I'd love to indulge in you frequently," he murmured with that intimate inflection that never failed to get to her. "But you're right, it is getting late."

Amanda accompanied him to the front door where she said, "Thanks."

"For the directional lesson?" he questioned, referring to their dalliance on the couch.

"For the offer to be my friend," she answered sincerely. "For leaving without a hassle."

Brady reached out to brush the back of his

hand across her cheek and drop a swift kiss onto her upturned lips. “Good night.”

Four days later Amanda was walking down the college’s front steps, heading for the faculty parking lot, when a voice hailed her from behind. Recognizing it as belonging to Guy Lox, she increased her pace but to no avail.

“Amanda, didn’t you hear me calling you?” he demanded peevishly, his breath coming in rapid little bursts because of his scramble down the stairs.

“I was on my way home, Professor.”

Guy’s eyes narrowed ominously at her cool dismissal. He was well aware of Amanda’s aversion to him and it grated on his inflated ego. “Come have a drink with me,” he pushed.

“She can’t,” another voice interceded on her behalf. “Amanda is going to give me a ride back to headquarters. Police business.”

“Sounds like funny business to me,” Guy muttered.

“Then it’s just as well we’re not asking you,” Brady smoothly returned, grasping Amanda’s arm and leading her toward the parking lot.

Guy stood fuming on the cement steps, furious at the turn of events. His ferret face wore a look that promised revenge as he pivoted and returned to the building.

Amanda and Brady had by this time reached the environs of the parking lot. “Where’s your car?” Brady paused to ask.

"It's over there." She pointed to the next aisle.

Brady headed toward a sedate sedan while Amanda walked up to the car beside it. "This one's mine," she pointed out, remembering for the first time that he'd never seen her car before because the red Porsche had always been safely tucked away in the garage.

Brady's low whistle of admiration was accompanied by a look of exaggerated disbelief. "This can't be Amanda's car!" he exclaimed.

"No? Then whose car is it?"

"Mandy's."

Amanda had to laugh at the lazy smugness of his voice. "You make it sound as though I have a split personality."

"Not split," he answered seriously. "I'd say more like divided — against yourself."

"I had no idea they taught clinical psychology at the police academy," she shot back, shaken by his accurate analysis.

"Clinical is not a term that applies in relation to you," Brady dryly returned.

Amanda made no reply as she unlocked the passenger door before striding around the low-slung hood to the driver's side.

"Are you sure you can handle all this horse-power?" Brady made the mistake of dubiously questioning as she slid behind the wheel.

"I'm going to drive the car, not carry it," was her tart rejoinder.

"You do have a sense of humor," he chuckled, suitably abashed.

"I'd have to around you," she tossed back.

"Librarians must make more than I thought," Brady mused.

Amanda shot him a startled look. "What makes you say that?"

"This Porsche." He patted the dashboard admiringly.

"I bought it used from one of the students when I first came to Deerfield."

"I'm relieved to hear that."

"Why?"

"Because I'd hate to think of you as being independently wealthy, or even close to it. The fact that you own your own house is bad enough."

"What's bad about that? Most men of my acquaintance find it a definite asset."

Brady cracked up. "I love the way you word things, Mandy. 'Men of my acquaintance,' " he repeated with a chuckle and a shake of his head.

"Why am I taking you to the police station?" she demanded in an annoyed tone. "Where's your car?"

"In for repairs."

"Both of them?"

"Yep."

"What would you have done if I hadn't come along? How would you have gotten back to the station then?" she questioned suspiciously.

"The same way I got out to the college, in a squad car. But then I would've had to come back to pick up my men. Besides, you looked like you needed saving from that joker."

Somehow Amanda doubted that Guy Lox would appreciate being called a joker. He took himself too seriously for that.

By this time they were in front of the police station, for it didn't take long to get from one place to another in a town the size of Deerfield!

Brady opened his seat belt before turning to her. "Thanks for the lift, Mandy." He playfully tugged on the renegade strands of honey-gold hair that had escaped her chignon. "I'll be seeing you."

But when she did see him it was in the presence of other people. Two more small fires had been discovered, both in the main administration building, and Brady was working overtime, devoting all his energy to the investigation. On the days she didn't see him in passing she was reminded of his existence by the continual speculations of her coworkers, while at night her dreams were filled with him.

Autumn's radiance had advanced into its mellow stage, but shades of unaccustomed melancholy dampened Amanda's Halloween. The neighborhood kids had been ringing the bell all afternoon. Caped wonders held their paper bags out for treats, chorusing their thank you's as Amanda dropped in miniature chocolate bars. This year there seemed to be an abundance of white-sheeted ghosts and hobos. "An accurate reflection on the state of the economy," was Amanda's pessimistic decision.

In an effort to capture some of the gaiety she saw in the children's faces, Amanda decided to bake a batch of chocolate chip cookies. She creamed the butter and sugar with angry strokes until her arm ached. Interrupted as she was by the constant summons of the front doorbell, it was no wonder that darkness had fallen by the time she put the first batch into the heated oven. Assuming that most of the neighborhood kids had already made their rounds, she was surprised to hear the doorbell ring yet again.

Grabbing a handful of candy, she pulled open the door. There, where she expected to find a group of costumed children, stood Brady. With his hands braced on either side of the door frame, he leaned forward to drop a kiss on her open lips. Amanda's reaction was unexpected. She tugged him over the threshold and into the house with a force that momentarily startled him.

"I had no idea you were so eager to see me, Mandy. If I'd known, I'd have come trick-or-treating sooner!"

Amanda's eyes glared her impatience. She knew from experience that the bright porch light illuminated the area so efficiently that it could have passed for a stage. "I don't like taking part in a neighborhood floor show."

"I understand," Brady nodded sagely. "You prefer the private showings."

Her exclamatory denial was overridden by Brady's curious, "What's that smell?"

"Oh, no," she wailed. "My cookies."

Brady followed her into the kitchen where he leaned against the countertop, watching her whisk one of the two cookie sheets out of the oven and onto a cooling rack. Unnerved by his leisurely perusal, she wasn't as cautious as usual while transferring the piping hot cookies and consequently burnt her finger.

"Ouch!" Amanda quickly lifted the injured finger, but Brady's hand shot out to change its destination from her mouth to his own where he rubbed the tip of his tongue over the reddened area.

"Better?" he asked. The movement of his lips shaping the words against her skin produced a rush of sensuous pleasure.

"Yes, thanks," was her shaky reply. Amanda removed her hand from further temptation before offering, "You can lick the spoon as a reward." She held the dough-covered utensil up to his lips.

"There's plenty here for two." Brady firmly grasped her wrist and invited, "Join me."

The spoon was like a giant lollypop between them. Under such close quarters, further contact was inevitable. It began with his lean finger swiping a chocolate chip from her chin and stealing it for himself.

"Hey," she protested. "That chocolate chip was on my side!"

"No, it wasn't," Brady took great pleasure in denying. "It was on your chin."

Amanda teasingly stuck out her tongue, whereupon Brady promptly placed a fingerful of batter on its pink tip. "There, now we're even."

"No, we're not." Amanda aimed her own

fingerful of dough at his chin, but was forced to abandon the mission when her hand was captured and guided to his lips. Once there, he seemed to take great pleasure out of dining on it, eventually drawing her entire finger into his mouth. The sensuous implication of his action incited a diffuse pleasure that rapidly spread through her.

His hand tunneled under her hair, impelling her forward. She knew what was coming and welcomed it with expectation. But Brady didn't merely kiss her; he tasted her, nibbling the succulent curve of her lower lip and relishing the sensitive inside corners before sipping the honeyed nectar within. This was just a foretaste of things to come. The sensual feast continued as his tongue tickled, savored, and toasted her. Amanda's soft murmurs proclaimed her pleasure, her pliant body indicative of her impassioned state.

The spoon soon lay forgotten on the table as Brady was otherwise occupied with pulling her closer. His hands traversed the curves of her body, nurturing her response and adorning her with delectable caresses. Amanda sighed and moved closer, her arms sliding under his vest to curve around his back. Unlike the first time she'd met him, there was no distraction of a gun to inhibit her explorations.

The thin cotton of his shirt did little to hide the rippling muscles of his back. Amanda was amazed at his remarkable solidness, the decisive breadth of his shoulders in comparison to the firm leanness of his waist. It was as though the maximum amount of power had been packed into the minimum amount of space, resulting in a muscular compactness that bespoke a man in excellent physical condition.

Heady from the magnitude of her reaction, Amanda buried her face in the curve of his neck, inhaling his clean male smell. It was a tangy muskiness mixed with . . . smoke? Her bemused eyes opened to slowly focus on the gray haze billowing from the oven.

"Oh, my God, the cookies!" Pulling away from him, she rushed to open the oven door. "They're burnt to a crisp!"

"So am I!" Brady returned with ragged humor.

Amanda didn't hear him, engrossed as she was with dumping the carbonized remains of the cookies in the garbage.

"It's no good crying over burnt cookies," he mockingly advised. "So why don't you open the surprise I brought you."

For the first time Amanda noticed the large paper bag sitting on the floor. "What is it?" she cautiously asked, not sure how many more surprises she could take in one day.

"Open it and see," he instructed, laughing at her expression of reluctance.

The bag's unexpected heaviness was explained when she opened it and found a large pumpkin inside.

"I noticed that you didn't have one sitting in your window." Brady's explanation was accompanied by a firm warning. "And don't you dare tell me that you're too old to be carving jack-o'-lanterns."

"I wasn't going to," she indignantly denied.

"Good." A congratulatory smile tugged on his lips. "Do you have some newspapers we could protect the table with?"

Amanda found some and supplied the other tools he needed, namely, a marker and a selection of sharp knives. Brady put her in charge of the artwork, with instructions to be as creative as possible.

Half an hour later the hollowed pumpkin had been transformed into a hilariously unbalanced jack-o'-lantern. Its teeth were the most prominent feature, due to the fact that Amanda had miscalculated and ended up with more teeth on one side than the other. The resultant lopsided growl looked more pathetic than frightening.

"Do you have a candle?" Brady asked.

"Why? So we can burn it?"

"How can you talk that way about your creation?"

Amanda slapped down the marker in disgust. "It looks ridiculous. I told you I wasn't any good at artwork."

"I disagree. You've captured that little man's entire personality."

"What little man?" she questioned in confusion.

"Lox. Don't you see the resemblance?"

Now that he pointed it out, there was a certain likeness! The realization made Amanda laugh until she was practically crying. Brady moved closer, wiping the mirthful tears from her cheeks. "You've got beautiful eyes," he murmured seductively. "They're the exact color of root beer Popsicles."

Expecting some poetic compliment, Brady's down-to-earth turn of phrase set her off again.

"What's so funny?" he demanded.

"You are," she choked.

"If that's the way you react to compliments, I may not give you any more."

"No, please go right ahead," she suppressed her laughter long enough to say. "My eyes are like Popsicles. How about my lips? What are they like? Cherry licorice?"

"I think I may have unleashed a monster," Brady muttered to himself, pulling her laughing figure into a tight embrace. "I hope you keep that smile reserved for me."

"Which smile?" she questioned.

"The one that warms your lips and adds sparkling carbonation to your root beer eyes!"

That cracked her up again.

Still holding her in a close embrace, Brady couldn't help but feel the gasp that punctuated her laughter. He rubbed the back of her head in confusion. "What was that?"

"I've got the . . . hiccups."

"Great. Come on, sit down." He led her over to a kitchen chair. "Where's your sugar bowl?"

"Over," hiccup, "there."

Brady pulled a teaspoon out of the drawer and

dipped it into the sugar bowl. "Here." He held the spoonful of sugar up to her lips. "Eat it."

"What for?"

"Just eat it," he instructed.

Amanda did so, grimacing slightly at the surplus of sweetness.

"There, your hiccups should be gone now."

She paused, waiting for the next jolt to rock her, but it didn't come. "It worked!"

" 'O ye of little faith,' " he berated her. "Of course it worked. Now that I've helped you, how about repaying the favor?"

"In what way?" she warily inquired.

"Don't worry, Mandy. I won't ask for anything you can't give," Brady promised, his intimate intonation running up and down her spine.

"What exactly did you have in mind?"

"How about a movie this weekend?" he surprised her by asking.

"A movie?" she echoed.

"Yes, a movie. Why? What did you have in mind?"

"Me?" She quickly shook her head. "Nothing."

His grin told her that he didn't believe her. He'd deliberately worded his invitation in such a way that she was bound to misinterpret his intentions. The naughty gleam in his eyes confirmed it.

Their ongoing battle of wits continued as Amanda planned her revenge. "I accept, providing I get to choose the movie."

Brady would live to regret his agreement. They

went to a Saturday matinee. That should have raised his suspicions, but the theater had several features playing, and he naturally assumed they'd be going to either the sophisticated thriller or the war-torn saga. Brady didn't receive the shock until they were in front of the theater and he asked which she'd prefer.

"*Fantasia.*"

He looked at her in dismay. "But that's Walt Disney."

"I know," she replied, joining the line in front of the box office.

Brady followed her, unequivocally stating, "There's no way I'm going to go see a Disney movie with a bunch of kids!"

"A deal's a deal, Brady." She moved forward a few steps as the line shortened. "You said I could pick the movie."

"This isn't fair."

"It's a great movie. You'll love it, you'll see." Her promise was accompanied by a reassuring pat on his arm.

Brady's speaking glance promised retribution at a later date. Once inside, Amanda was all set to head for the concession stand when Brady suddenly grabbed her hand and practically dragged her across the lobby.

"What's the matter?" she gasped, breathless from running to keep up with him.

"Nothing," he denied in the darkened interior of the theater. "I just wanted to make sure we got our seats before they're all taken."

He didn't slow his pace as he hurried down the aisle and hustled her into a center row. Furtively looking over his shoulder, he quickly chose a seat and impatiently tugged her down beside him.

Amanda eyed Brady's slouching form in confusion. He really was acting most peculiarly. "Aren't you going to take your coat off?"

"No." He pulled up the collar, partially shielding his face.

"Brady, are you all right?"

"No."

"What's wrong?"

"I'm never going to be able to live this down," he muttered in disgust.

"Live what —" she began when a booming voice interrupted her.

"Gallagher! I thought I recognized you."

Brady straightened with fatalistic resignation. "Chief," he acknowledged, standing up.

"This is the last place I would have expected to find you," the police chief stated. "My kids wanted to see the movie, so I brought them. And you?"

"Amanda wanted to see the picture," he explained before making the introductions. "Amanda, this is Police Chief Jabowski. Chief, this is Amanda Richards."

"Glad to meet you, Amanda. I never knew you had such good taste, Gallagher!" The police chief's aside was accompanied with a jab of his elbow. "Well, I see my kids have found a seat in the third row, so I'd better go. Nice meeting you, Amanda."

Amanda made some suitable rejoinder, trying not to grin at Brady's discomfited expression. "I'm sorry, Brady," she apologized once the chief was out of earshot. "I didn't know your boss would be here."

Brady made no comment. Instead, he casually draped his arm around her shoulder, figuratively picking up the gauntlet she'd thrown down. "There's more than one way to win a war, Mandy. And this is one war I do plan on winning!"

Chapter Six

It's no problem, Dean Routledge," the head librarian assured the college official over the phone in front of a fuming Amanda. "The library would be more than willing to host the faculty wine and cheese party. We'll certainly put on a show for you, sir."

Amanda almost blew a fuse. What John meant was that the staff would put out all the work and he would take all the credit, as usual. Since the faculty lounge was closed for repairs, they should hold the monthly faculty party in the cafeteria, or skip it altogether for November, but not impose on the already overburdened library. The moment the head librarian hung up the phone, Amanda launched into her argument.

"John, with the handicaps the library is working under, I really don't think it's wise to offer our services for any extra work."

"This won't be work, Amanda. It's recreation of a sort. Everyone loves a party, and it will be great for the staff's morale. After all, you were the one who told me that morale was at an all-time low."

"That's true, but —"

"I think it's due to the anxiety about that arsonist," John interrupted. "I can't believe the police still haven't come up with anything in their investigation. Another example of our tax dollars being wasted."

"The police are doing the best they can." Amanda defended Brady's investigation.

"I'm sure they are," John agreed in a tone that clearly voiced his opinion of their competence, or lack of it.

"You can't blame the library's problems on the arsonist, John. We're short-staffed, and the cut in funds for student help was the last straw."

"There's nothing I can do about it, Amanda."

"You could go to the dean and ask him to approve filling our vacant positions."

"You don't understand the politicking that has to go into these matters. By having the party here in the library, we'll be softening the dean, so he'll give us what we want."

Amanda gave up in despair. John Abbington already knew what he thought. He didn't want to be confused with facts. But things would certainly change after his retirement, when she was in charge!

The faculty party traditionally fell on the second Friday of the month and was scheduled to begin at four. Although originally designed solely for the professors, all staff members were now invited. Since Technical Services had the largest office, it was chosen for the party site. Their long work table had been cleared and was now protected by a paper tablecloth. On top of that was spread an array of crackers and Wisconsin cheeses. The wine punch hid a multitude of sins, which is why Amanda avoided it. Her eyes were already glaring over John's repeated raids on the food. "Look at him, standing there gorging himself. He hasn't done a damn thing to help with all this."

"Here, try one of these." Beth stuck a cracker into Amanda's mouth, hoping to forestall a scene. "I meant to tell you that I really like your outfit."

Amanda automatically glanced down at the olive-and-red patterned blouse that was tucked into a red wool skirt.

"With your willowy figure you can wear those slim skirts. I'm too short," Beth complained.

"You're not too short, Beth. You're petite. I feel about as poised as a giraffe next to you."

Beth giggled. "Sorry, I can't see the resemblance. Maybe it's the Calvin Klein belt that's blocking my vision. It is Calvin, isn't it?"

"Yes," Amanda confirmed, fingering the butter-soft leather belt.

"They cost a packet."

"I know. The danger connected with this kind of thing is . . ."

"That it could become a habit!" Beth interjected.

"Besides that," Amanda laughed. "The real problem is that it's so nice and so expensive that you don't want to wear it!"

"I know," Beth agreed. "You remember that expensive skirt I bought last year? I still haven't worn it. I keep waiting for some special occasion.

I'm afraid to wear it out on a dinner date in case I spill something and ruin it. So it just hangs in my closet. Every so often I take it out and gaze at it adoringly before putting it back."

"I know the feeling. What I finally had to do was forget how much I paid for it and simply enjoy it. After all, clothes aren't a commodity that you can store in the closet and have increase in value, like money in the bank."

"Even money in the bank doesn't do that in these times of high inflation!" Beth humorously retorted.

Since the library staff had the least distance to travel, they were the first to arrive. Other administrators, staff, and faculty members began drifting in soon afterward. Beth and Amanda were joined by Helen and Susan, both of whom had cups of punch in their hands. With customary promptness, Susan soon brought the conversation around to the subject of men.

"There aren't any cute guys in this year's senior class," she bemoaned. "At least not unmarried ones."

"I don't understand how men can be cute," Helen protested. "Men can be good-looking or handsome, but not cute."

"Look, I'll give you some examples," Susan offered, taking another sip of the potent punch. "Robert Redford is handsome."

"He's perfect," Beth sighed.

"He's left-handed," was Amanda's contribution.

"Now, Baryshnikov, on the other hand, is cute," Susan continued.

"And is Brady handsome or cute?" Helen wanted to know.

Amanda had no intention of volleying that one, which left the field open for Susan. Emboldened by the alcohol content of the punch, Susan ignored the obvious signs of her boss's displeasure and gave her considered opinion. "Brady's not pretty-boy handsome . . ."

"He's not a boy at all," Amanda muttered under her breath, resisting the sudden desire to throttle Susan as she continued. "I'd say Brady's good-looking in a cute sort of way."

"I still say ruggedly handsome sounds better," Helen maintained. "Cute makes him sound like a teddy bear."

Susan grinned rapaciously. "I wouldn't mind taking him to bed with me!"

Helen, sensing the anger emanating from Amanda, tried to get the conversation moving again by volunteering, "Tyrone Power was always my favorite. And Errol Flynn." She sighed expressively. "He had such a wickedly naughty gleam in his eye."

"You mean he was sexy." This from Susan, of course.

"That's not what we called it in those days," Helen resisted.

"Isn't that what you meant?" Susan challenged.

"I suppose, although it was something more than just beefcake. It's an elusive, almost intangible, asset that some men have — in the way they look at a woman, in their confident assumption of masculinity. I don't know how else to describe it, except to say that Brady Gallagher's got it!"

Amanda was shocked. She'd expect a statement like that from Susan, but not from a sixty-year-old grandmother!

As if reading her thoughts, Susan piped up with, "It's those bedroom eyes of his and that virile body!" She sighed expressively. "He'd be worth going to jail for!"

Amanda excused herself from the group, quietly fuming at Susan's provocative comments. She'd had to bite her tongue to stop from asking if Susan thought Brady worth getting fired for, because she'd been damn tempted to give Susan the ax then and there! So engrossed with her own thoughts was she that Guy Lox's arrival went unnoticed. Had she caught his leering glances, her skin would have shuddered in revulsion.

Guy waited, feeding his courage with numerous cups of punch, uncouthly dipping his glass into the liquid instead of using the serving ladle. He timed his approach so that Amanda was alone, segregated from the rest of the merrymaking crowd.

Amanda's first indication of his presence was an alcohol-laden voice slurring over her shoulder. "I wanna talk to you!"

"Not right now, Professor," she coldly refused.

"Where are you goin'?" Guy demanded truculently at Amanda's involuntary movement of escape. His hand shot out, thick stubby fingers closing with sickening strength around her upper arm.

Her temper already frayed, Amanda warned, "I'm not in the mood for a hassle, Professor!"

"S'right, baby. I know what you are in the mood for."

"Let go of me," Amanda frigidly demanded. "Now!"

It was the wrong approach to take. She became aware of that immediately. Guy grew even more belligerent. Pressing oppressively closer, he muttered obscenities into her ear, his panting breath contaminating her neck, his bulging frame defiling her body.

Genuinely frightened now, Amanda tried to jerk away, wincing as Guy's fingers tightened painfully. She was about ready to kick him in the shins, or higher if necessary, when for once in his life John Abbington did something useful. "There you are, Guy. I've been meaning to talk to you."

While Guy's attention was momentarily diverted, Amanda grabbed at the chance to free herself from his loathsome touch. She suppressed the waves of nausea threatening to overwhelm her, and quickly made her way to the exit. Out in the deserted hallway, tremors of alarm forced her to stop and lean against the wall. She was drawing in great gulps of air, when a hand suddenly cupped her elbow. Her body immediately stiffened in preparation for a fight, adrenaline pumping through her system.

"Mandy?" a deep voice whispered in her ear, repeating it in alarm when she turned and threw her arms around her rescuer's neck, burrowing close as if seeking protection.

Brady immediately knew something was wrong. Amanda was not the kind of woman to indulge in public displays of emotion. Recognizing that she wouldn't want to be seen while in such a state, he urged her into an empty conference room farther along the hallway.

"What is it? What happened?" he demanded.

"Just hold me a minute." Her quivering voice was muffled by the thick material of Brady's vest, but he heard it all the same.

"Sure. I thought you'd never ask," he gently teased, his strong arms tenderly enfolding her within their protective clasp. He held her close to his heart, gently rocking her to and fro. His embrace offered both safety and comfort. Amanda closed her eyes and rested her head on his shoulder. After a few moments of this treatment she self-consciously stepped away.

Brady eased his clasp slightly, but still kept Amanda ensnared in a loose embrace. "You don't have to move away," he protested with that special smile she'd come to know. It made her feel the center of his world. "Feel better?"

She nodded. "I'm sorry I made such a fool of myself."

"There's nothing foolish about wanting me to

hold you. In fact I think it shows a marked sign of intelligence!" Switching from teasing humor to seriousness, Brady went on to quietly ask, "What happened?"

"It was nothing."

"Come on, Mandy. Although I would love it, you don't fall into my arms for no reason. What upset you? Someone at the party have a little too much to drink?"

Amanda's startled jerk gave her away.

"I see. Who was it?" he demanded, his voice grim with determination.

Amanda could feel the anger emanating from him. Brady never did things by half measures, and frankly she was almost as frightened about what he might do to Guy as she had been of the sleazy professor himself. Brady's solution might be a case of the cure being worse than the illness. He'd probably barge into the gathering and floor Guy. While that scenario did have its appeal, Amanda knew it would only make matters worse. Besides, shaken as she was, she didn't think she could handle another scene.

"Please, let's forget it. I probably read more into it than really existed," she said, wishing that had been the case but knowing it wasn't.

"Are you sure?" he questioned, glancing down at her pale face.

"Yes, I'm sure. What are you doing here anyway?"

"The dean invited me to the party. Although why he should after the mess this investigation is in, I don't know." Brady's voice reflected his impatient disgust.

Glad to get off the subject of herself, Amanda commiserated. "Aren't things going well?"

"Not very. I suppose it could be worse, at least there haven't been any more fires for almost two weeks now. But enough shop talk." Amanda felt the loss as he released her from his embrace. "Go get your things."

"Why?"

"Because I'm taking you home." Seeing her indecisive expression, he added, "It's after five; you've put in your time."

"It's not a matter of just putting in my time," she protested.

"I know. Your devotion to your profession is great. But right now I'm taking you home. Let's go."

Actually Amanda was relieved to be getting away. They met Beth in the hallway and Brady told her they were leaving. While still quite shaken, Amanda insisted on driving herself home.

"You just want to make sure your baby gets to bed tonight," Brady teased, patting the Porsche's smooth lines.

For the life of her, she couldn't come up with a snappy reply. She felt that if she showed any signs of unbending, she'd break down completely, and she already felt foolish for literally crying on Brady's shoulder. So she kept her mask in place, automatically following her route home. It was only when she pulled into her driveway that she realized she had no clear recollection of which route she'd taken, the shortcut or the alternate. It was rather frightening to see how completely she'd put herself on automatic, blocking out all incoming messages.

Amanda was still sitting in the Porsche when Brady pulled his Mustang up alongside a moment later. Darkness hid his worried expression from her as he hurried over to open her car door. By the time he leaned down to speak to her, his expression had resumed its customary amusement. "Were you waiting for valet service?"

Amanda recollected her wandering thoughts and accepted his helping hand.

"How about a nice glass of sherry to calm your nerves," Brady suggested as soon as they were inside.

Belatedly recalling her duties as a hostess, Amanda removed her coat. "That'd be nice. And what would you like?"

"Besides you?"

His obvious attempt to cheer her up brought a half-smile to her lips. "I'm not on the menu."

"Speaking of menus, how about if I make dinner for you tonight?"

"I don't have much food in the house," she warned.

"As long as you've got eggs. I make a mean omelet."

"Okay. The kitchen's all yours. I've never had a mean omelet before." The words were teasing, but the delivery lacked enthusiasm.

Half an hour later they sat down to a simple, but tasty meal. Brady had refused to allow Amanda in her own kitchen and she hadn't pushed it. He found a bottle of wine in the refrigerator, which they were lingering over now.

"What are your plans for Thanksgiving?" Brady asked.

"Thanksgiving," she repeated with mild haziness. Her mouth had been incredibly dry, so she'd been partaking freely of the wine.

"Yes, Thanksgiving. You know, turkey, pumpkin pie, Pilgrims, and all that jazz."

"Did you like that movie?" she threw him by asking.

"What movie?" His face was a study of masculine bewilderment.

"All That Jazz."

Brady didn't get the connection. "We were talking about Thanksgiving."

"I don't like holidays."

"I'm getting that impression," he ruefully acknowledged. "Why not?"

But Amanda just shook her head and refused to answer.

"Okay, if you won't tell me, I'll have to tell you what my plans are. Unfortunately I'm scheduled to work, otherwise I'd have invited you to our house for Thanksgiving. My mom always cooks enough for an army. In fact, when I was in the army she sent me a Care package full of canned cranberry relish and Oreo cookies!"

Brady went on to relate more funny anecdotes

about previous Thanksgivings, including his younger sister's first attempt at cooking a turkey. He talked about his family with a warm affection that she found surprising in a man.

"You never did tell me what your plans were for the holiday," he reminded her during a lull in the conversation.

"Beth's invited me over to her parents' house. They're nice people."

"Unlike your own parents?" he astutely guessed.

The shock she'd experienced earlier at the party must have used up a lot of her reserves, because for a moment Amanda found herself wanting to confide in Brady, to tell him what it was like growing up with two people who were too wrapped up in their own lives to give a damn about a child. But she hesitated to reveal too much, to lay herself open for ridicule. So she glossed over her true feelings, said a few glib excuses, and moved on to another topic of conversation.

Brady followed her lead, noting the shadows of vulnerability in her eyes. She'd been through some type of ordeal already today and he didn't intend to push her in any way. They talked until far into the night, sharing common outlooks on life.

When Brady noticed her drooping eyes and caught her yawning he took her by the hand and pulled her up from the couch. "Come on," he instructed. "It's time you were in bed."

Amanda mistakenly thought that Brady was accompanying her to the foot of the stairs whereupon he would go one way, out the front door, and she another, upstairs to bed. Instead, he started guiding her drowsy body up the stairs. "Where do you think you're going?" she stopped in her tracks to demand.

"I thought you might need some help undressing for bed."

"I can undress myself, thank you," she retorted.

"Then go on." His hand nudged her along encouragingly. "I'll bring you up a cup of hot cocoa in a few minutes."

Her words of protest were cut off by Brady's "Consider it part of my catering service."

Amanda was conservatively covered by a red velour robe when Brady knocked. "Room service," he announced, pushing the door open with his foot.

She took the proffered mug, sipping at it appreciatively. "Thanks."

Brady thoughtfully eyed the top of her lowered head. Despite her tiredness there was still an air of brittle tension about her. Coming to a sudden decision, he straightened his broad shoulders and put out a hand to take the empty mug from her grasp. "Good night, Mandy. Sleep well."

"Good night, Brady. And thanks."

"I'll see you tomorrow, Mandy," he promised.

The rolling drumbeat of a Fleetwood Mac song abruptly interrupted a nightmare Amanda was having about Guy. Her eyes flew open to check the time, her hand automatically reaching out to press the snooze bar of the clock radio. Seven thirty! Why had she set the alarm for seven thirty on a Saturday? Her sleep-ridden mind was unable to come up with a suitable explanation. Amanda turned over with a groan. She hadn't had a good night; her sleep had been constantly broken by dreams that left her on edge. Her head was still thick and her tongue felt like an army had marched over it. Realizing that she hadn't brushed her teeth after drinking the cocoa last night, Amanda shoved off the bed covers and silently padded across the hall to the bathroom. Since she was alone she didn't bother with a robe.

Standing barefoot before the sink, Amanda groggily shoved her hair out of her eyes and stared at the mirror. But her thoughts weren't on its reflection, they were on Brady and how nice he'd been last night. She squeezed toothpaste onto her brush with mechanical disinterest. Eyes forward, she stuck her toothbrush into her mouth and brushed. Still not paying attention, she turned on the tap and filled the water glass without looking down. It wasn't until she'd lifted the glass to her lips that she caught the glimmer of something moving.

Tearing her eyes away from the mirror, she saw a huge black spider only a bare inch away from her lips! It was rapidly pulling itself out of the water and crawling up over the rim of her glass. Amanda's scream shattered the air as surely as the dropped glass shattered on the floor.

The spider landed safely in the sink.

There was a pounding of footsteps on the stairs and then Brady literally burst onto the scene, the splinters of glass crunching under his leather boots. "Mandy! What's going on?"

Her trembling finger pointed to the spider malevolently staring at her from the edge of the sink. Amanda scrunched her eyes closed while Brady swiftly dispatched it down the drain. Her eyes flew open again as she felt herself lifted and her flailing hands came in contact with his bare shoulders.

Realizing for the first time the reality of his presence, she squirmed indignantly. "What are you doing here?"

"You scared the hell out of me," he gruffly accused her, carrying her across the hallway to her room and depositing her on the bed.

"Well, what do you think that spider did to me?"

"I can't imagine," he mocked dryly. "Did you hurt yourself on the broken glass?"

"No, I don't think so."

"Let's check, shall we?" Instead of kneeling before her in a gallant pose, Brady sat on the bed beside her and hooked his fingers around her ankle, lifting it so high that she was thrown back onto the mattress.

Her muttered references to his high-handed bedside manner were ignored as he probed the sole of her bare foot for glass splinters.

"What are you doing here this early?" she demanded, wriggling her toes at the tickling sensations running up her leg. Was Brady doing that intentionally? She lifted her head to check, but could discern no answer from his deliberately deadpan expression.

"I never left." His stark reply knocked all thoughts of teasing out of her mind.

"You mean you spent the night . . ."

". . . downstairs on your sofa. Yes."

"But why?"

"I didn't think you'd let me share your bed."

She dismissed his mocking humility. "I meant why did you stay."

"Because you were upset."

"You needn't have bothered. And you don't have to hold my foot that high just to look at it," she protested, leaning forward to frantically grab the bottom hem of her negligee.

Her new pose revealed a generous amount of creamy curvature to Brady's more than appreciative gaze. "You look good in blue, Mandy. And pink," he added as her cheeks reddened.

That's a flush of anger, she assured herself, *not embarrassment. Don't let him get away with this!*

"What's your mother going to think, since you didn't go home last night?" Her haughty words were meant to make Brady feel like a teenage boy who'd missed curfew.

"I imagine she'll come after you and demand that you make an honest man out of me!" he returned easily, refusing to rise to the bait.

"You never take anything seriously," she accused, jerking her unharmed feet away from him.

"I'd like to take you, Mandy. Seriously, or any other way I could get you!"

Amanda didn't pause to think; she reacted instinctively. Grabbing her pillow, she thumped him with it. She heard the whoosh of oxygen exit from his lungs as the pillow struck him right across the ribs. Amanda's spurt of anger was overcome by a wave of concern. "Did I hurt you?" she questioned anxiously.

Distracted by her concern, she didn't realize Brady's intention until he'd tugged the pillow out of her hands and swiped her with it.

"That's not fair!"

"All's fair . . ."

". . . in love and war, I know." She stopped her struggles long enough to ask, "Which is this, Brady?"

"You tell me," he challenged.

"Right now I think it's a pillow fight!" She grabbed another pillow from behind her and threw it, but Brady was no longer sitting where he'd been a moment ago.

"Shame, shame. You've jettisoned all your ammunition, Mandy. Not very bright," he chided her while advancing toward her, holding his feathery weapon ready to throw. Mandy retreated until she was backed up against the headboard. She turned to flee from the bed, but in that moment Brady caught her, successfully pinning her to the mattress.

Remembering that the best defense is a good offense, Amanda regally demanded, "Well? Do you give up yet?"

She could feel the laughter rippling through the bare chest hovering above her. "You're the only woman I know who, in the face of defeat, would demand my surrender."

"I didn't demand anything. I was merely asking a question."

"Then, no, I don't give up. I'm never giving up on you." His expressive look took warm nibbles out of her poise, making her feel warm and shivery inside. "How about it, Mandy? Is the war over?"

"I don't know," she whispered. "Sometimes you make me so mad I could hit you."

"I noticed."

"Then there are other times when I . . ."

"When you what?" he prompted, stroking her face with the palm of his hand.

"Never mind."

"Ve have vays of making you talk!" Brady's warning was delivered in a stormtrooper's voice.

"You drive me crazy, do you know that?"

Brady lowered his head to whisper in her ear. "I know I get to you, the same way you get to me."

Her ensuing fit of giggles made him draw away. "That wasn't meant to be funny," he informed her with rueful indignation.

"I can't help it. I'm ticklish," she tried to explain.

"You are?" Brady exclaimed with fiendish glee. "Where?"

His exploring hands boldly went in search of her funnybone, their magical touch barely registered in one location before moving on to another. Her fingers chased after his, but he was faster than she and eluded her.

"I told you I was ambidextrous," he reminded her.

"I'm not ticklish in any of those places!" she gasped. "I'm ticklish when you whisper in my ear."

"That's a pity. Then I won't be able to whisper sweet nothings to you. After all, I wouldn't want a fit of laughter, or, even worse, hiccups, interrupting our lovemaking. And speaking of sweet nothings, I think that's a very good description of what you're wearing. What's it made of?" The question may have been conversational, but the intonation most definitely was not.

Concentrating with difficulty, she replied, "I don't know."

"Feels good," he told her.

Her strangled yes wasn't referring to the material but to the way his hands felt as they glided across the topography of her body. While those hands inaugurated the fun and games, his wandering lips did the follow-up work, mapping the planes of her face with sensual detail and intermittently returning to the inviting delectability of her mouth. *I'll stop this in a minute,* she assured herself. Amanda's fingers fanned out into his dark curls, her palms molded to the shape of his head. Their tongues were soon engaged in a languid tangle that stoked the liquid flames consuming her.

By carefully sliding the spaghetti straps of her nightgown out of the way, Brady opened new territory to his sensuous survey. His teasing tongue brushed across the bare canvas of her shoulder, the potent stimulation inducing a rush of dizzy euphoria. Without the support of the straps, the lace bodice slid provocatively lower, displaying more than it concealed. Amanda's breath was now coming in short gasps, which further threatened the tenuous position of her neckline.

Emulating Brady by exploring his body the way he was exploring hers, she was unprepared for the elemental enjoyment she derived from touching him. His groan of pleasure at the touch of her hands brought a smile of satisfaction to her lips, and her eyes glowed with the knowledge that she excited him. Amanda became bolder, her tantalizing fingers loitering around the warm flesh of his waist. His bare skin was smooth yet rough, soft yet firm. Her provocative fingers dipped to slide over the taut denim covering his thighs, setting up a chain reaction of thermal warmth that threatened a complete meltdown.

They were a motion away from setting forth on an irrevocable course when the phone on Amanda's bedside table let out a shrill peal. Brady groaned against her smooth curvaceousness, his arms momentarily tightening before he released her with a frustrated sigh. "You'd better get that."

Amanda reached for the receiver with a trembling hand, her eyes on the rippling muscles of Brady's bare torso as he rolled onto his back.

Her voice sounded hoarse as she mumbled, "Hello."

She paused a moment and then handed the phone to Brady. "It's for you."

He took the receiver, trapping her behind the coiled phone cord. Amanda ducked under it and escaped the tempting confines of the bed. She pulled on the red velour robe she'd worn last night and firmly belted it just as the doorbell rang.

"Damn," she muttered under her breath, hurrying down the stairs.

"Hi, Amanda," Beth greeted her once the door was open. "Ready to go to Leeman's sale?"

Amanda's face reflected her guilty dismay. She'd forgotten all about agreeing to accompany Beth to the store's annual early morning sale.

"Oh!" Beth's eyes and mouth both resembled that rounded letter of the alphabet.

Amanda turned to see what her friend was staring at. Of course it was Brady, cheerfully traipsing down the stairs minus his shirt.

"This isn't as bad as it looks," Amanda began.

"Good morning, Beth," Brady greeted her with no sign of Amanda's evident embarrassment. He'd crossed the hallway and already shrugged into his shirt before Beth collected herself sufficiently to reply. "Morning, Brady."

"As much as I'd love to stay and talk to you, I've got to get to work." He paused on his way out the door to drop a swift kiss on Amanda's startled lips. "I'll talk to you later," he promised with unconcealed relish.

Chapter Seven

Amanda!"

Beth's insistent voice brought Amanda's eyes back from Brady's fast-departing figure.

"I'm sorry if I interrupted something," her friend continued. "You told me to come by at eight thirty and pick you up."

"You didn't interrupt anything," Amanda stated, not entirely untruthfully. The phone call was actually responsible for interrupting something. How had the police department known where to find Brady? Had he told everyone in Deerfield that he was spending the night with her? It sure felt like it! Amanda's expression darkened ominously as she reviewed the blithe way he'd made his departure, leaving her to correct all the wrong impressions.

"When I get my hands on him . . ."

Amanda didn't realize she'd muttered the angry words out loud until she heard her friend's teasing, "I'm sure he can hardly wait!"

"Beth!"

Beth was unrepentant. "Amanda, it's obvious from the way Brady looks at you."

"What is?"

"That he's crazy about you."

"He's crazy all right," Amanda agreed in an

undertone. “He spent the night on the couch!”

“That makes him crazy?”

“Of course it does.”

“Why? Where did you plan on having him spend the night?”

“I didn’t plan it at all!”

“I see.” Beth nodded understandingly. “It just happened.”

“Nothing happened, or almost nothing,” she amended.

“Sounds more like something almost happened. So tell me before I die of curiosity. How did you coerce Deerfield’s sexiest cop into sleeping on your couch?”

“I didn’t coerce him,” Amanda indignantly protested. “It was entirely his idea!”

“Then I’m disappointed in him,” Beth sighed. “Those bedroom eyes of his must he deceptive!”

“No, they’re not.” Amanda spoke without thinking.

“Then why was he on the couch?”

“Look, it’s all really very simple. Someone at the party yesterday came on a little strong and upset me. Brady happened by when I was still shaken up about it. Apparently he got this crazy notion to spend the night down here. He didn’t want me to be alone while I was in what he perceived as an ‘emotional state.’ ”

“Who says chivalry is dead?”

“Must be the same person who put that spider in my water glass.” There she went again, muttering her thoughts aloud.

"In your water glass? Gross!" Beth shuddered.

"Brady killed it." Amanda felt a momentary twinge of guilt about the octoped's demise and hoped its relatives wouldn't come after her thirsting for revenge!

"Not only does he sleep on couches, but he also kills spiders!" Beth marveled in pretended awe. "I'd snatch him up if I were you, Amanda. A model like that is bound to be much in demand!"

Amanda turned Beth's words around. "A model like that is also bound to demand much!"

"Mmm, but think what you'd get in return."

Amanda had thought about it, that's what worried her. Maybe it would help if she talked about it with Beth, marshalled her defences and presented them in a reasonable way.

"Are you really set on going to Leeman's sale today?" Amanda asked.

"Not if you'd rather talk." Beth checked her watch. "All the good bargains have probably gone by now anyway."

"I'm sorry."

"Don't be. I'd only have run up my charge account."

"Okay. Then let me go get dressed."

"And I'll make us some coffee," Beth offered. "I haven't eaten anything yet today, and my stomach feels like a bottomless pit."

While she was upstairs Amanda swept up the broken glass that littered the bathroom floor. She came back downstairs dressed in a pair of gabardine slacks and an olive knit sweater.

Beth had the butcherblock table all set, the coffeepot and a dish of danish in the center. "I don't know why you keep fighting it," she began, before Amanda was even seated.

"Fighting what?"

"The way you feel about Brady."

Amanda swallowed a bite of sweet roll. "I'm not sure how I feel about him," she finally confessed.

"That's a switch! You always seem to know exactly what your feelings are. You've never shown the least tendency toward uncertainty before."

"I've never met anyone like Brady before."

"He is a hunk," Beth sighed.

"So Susan keeps telling me," Amanda dryly returned.

"It's true. But he's also a nice guy."

"Beth, I have no intention of getting involved with a young cop!" Amanda coolly informed her.

"Young?" Beth challenged.

"Well . . . younger," Amanda qualified.

"So what's wrong with that? I'm younger than you are, and we get along fine."

"It's all right for friends to be younger," Amanda tried to explain.

"But not lovers?" Beth irrepressibly inquired.

"Brady is not my lover!" *At least not yet,* an inner voice silently mocked.

"What's wrong? Don't you think you can handle Brady? Because if that's the case, then you're seriously underestimating yourself, Amanda. I think you two are made for each other. And so does Helen."

"Helen?"

"Sure. And how can you argue with our resident matchmaker?"

"I seem to recall you arguing with her when she tried to fix you up with her nephew from Minneapolis."

"That's different. He was impossible."

"So's Brady!" Amanda maintained.

"But not in the same way."

"No, not in the same way," she acknowledged, remembering Helen's nephew. "But impossible all the same."

"What exactly is it about him that aggravates you so much?"

"There are so many things."

"But I'll bet you can't think of a single example."

Beth was right. Now that Amanda had been given the opportunity, she couldn't pinpoint any one thing that exasperated her. Brady deliberately embarrassed her, but she'd sound like an idiot if she admitted that that bothered her.

"Does his being a cop upset you?" Beth prompted.

"I'm not sure."

"There you go again. You seem sure enough that you don't want to get involved with Brady, but completely at sea as to why!"

"We don't have anything in common."

"Then why do you have so much fun with him?"

Amanda sighed, moodily staring at the contents of her half-empty coffee cup. "I've asked myself that a million times."

"Maybe you're so busy asking that you haven't stopped to listen," Beth discerningly suggested. "My advice to you is this: Stop worrying! Just sit back and enjoy it. See what happens."

Amanda remembered her friend's words long after she'd left. They came back to her while she was sorting laundry, cleaning the refrigerator, even while microwaving her frozen dinner. When the phone rang she hoped the call would take her mind off the disturbing detective. It did no such thing.

"How was your day, Mandy?" Brady's warm voice questioned over the telephone line.

"Fine," was her automatic answer. "And yours?"

"It could've been better."

"It must be tough working on weekends," Amanda commiserated with overblown sympathy.

"It was tougher leaving you this morning!"

"It was hard on me too, Brady," she purred. "I could hardly restrain myself." Her grin took on a measure of satisfaction as she registered the unsteadiness of Brady's indrawn breath. Here was her chance to get even!

"Restrain yourself from what?" he pressed, wanting to hear more.

"From clobbering you!"

"Not exactly the response I was hoping for," Brady murmured wryly.

"Look, I appreciate your concern for me, which you showed by staying the night. But it really wasn't necessary, and I resent the way you embarrassed me in front of Beth."

"How about a deal, Mandy. I'll stop embarrassing you if you'll stop denying what's between us."

"Brady, I'm not sure what there is between us." Amanda found it easier to discuss their relationship over the phone. This way there was only the warmth of Brady's voice, without the reinforcing impact of his caressive glances.

"But you are willing to admit there is something?"

"Yes, there is something."

"Then why don't you stop fighting it?" His voice reached out to her. "I won't hurt you, Mandy."

"Not intentionally, perhaps."

"Just keep in mind that you have an equal influence over me."

"I do?" Amanda sounded doubtful.

"Yes, you do." There wasn't a hint of hesitation in his ready affirmation.

"Oh." She paused a moment, digesting this new piece of information.

Laughing softly, Brady queried, "That all you've got to say?"

"No, I've got a lot more to say, but I'm not sure how to say it."

"You're being cautious again," he gently chastised.

"Maybe it's because I've never felt this way before."

"Scary, isn't it?"

His words astonished her. "For you too?"

"Sure. A cop getting mixed up with a fierce librarian. You've got to admit, it sounds a bit far out."

Had she ever noticed how readily Brady laughed at himself, or had she been too busy getting "het up," as he said, because he was laughing at her?

"Is this your way of telling me that books and badges don't mix?" she teased.

"I wouldn't want to take credit for that line," he denied with a groan, before continuing on a more serious note. "We're in this together, Mandy, and I'm no more certain of where we're going than you are." His tone was one of tender irony.

"Is that meant to be reassuring?"

"No. I wasn't trying to be reassuring, just honest. Would you rather be scared alone?"

"Since misery loves company, fright must as well."

"So is it a deal?" he pressed.

"Is what a deal?"

"I'll stop embarrassing you if you'll stop running away."

"We've been acting like a couple of kids, haven't we?" she murmured.

"I don't know about that," Brady mused. "I

can recall several occasions when we were acting like adults engaged in adult activities, and enjoying every minute of it!"

"But now we'll have no more game-playing."

"Oh, I wouldn't go that far," he denied. "Let's just say we're advancing to the next level of difficulty!"

The conversation marked a subtle shift in their relationship. Amanda attempted to come to terms with her feelings for Brady and he refrained from embarrassing her in public. She learned that with Brady, diplomacy accomplished more than confrontation. Surprisingly enough, Brady discovered the same thing about her!

By Thanksgiving a snowfall of several inches covered the countryside, softening the harsh lines of the starkly barren trees and disguising the surrounding landscape. When Brady discovered that Amanda had never learned how to ice skate, he insisted on teaching her. Due to record cold temperatures, the smaller lakes were already frozen over. They chose one a couple miles west of town, avoiding the more popular recreational areas in favor of a secluded setting.

Amanda was relieved; she had no desire to make a fool of herself in front of a lot of people. Besides, she doubted her ability to stay out of other people's way while trying to stay upright. She could do one, or the other, but not both!

"I could've taught you how to skate down on the lake by the college," Brady said, his tone

one of barely restrained amusement. "We didn't have to come all the way out here to Indian Lake."

"Oh, yes, we did. This state has almost fifteen thousand inland lakes, so you can't say it's been difficult finding one. I have no intention of making a spectacle of myself in front of a bunch of laughing students!"

"You can make a spectacle of yourself in front of me anytime," he offered.

Amanda had to laugh at his boyishly hopeful expression. "You'll see me make an idiot of myself soon enough."

Brady began the skating lesson as soon as their boots were exchanged for ice skates. "We'll concentrate on standing up first. On the count of three, okay?"

Amanda nodded.

"One, two, three!"

She got up and nearly fell down again, hanging on to Brady in alarm. Now she knew what a newborn colt must feel like, with spindly legs going out in all different directions.

"Steady," Brady murmured. "I've got you."

After a few minutes Amanda got accustomed to a sharp edge supporting her instead of a flat surface, and they slowly made their way out onto the icebound lake. Brady went first, turning around and holding out his hands to her. She wrapped her gloved fingers around his and let him pull her along.

"Keep your legs straight. I'll pull you around so you can get a feel for the ice."

She followed his instructions, enjoying the sensation of gliding across the smooth surface.

"You're doing fine!" he praised her. "Now try moving your legs like this." He showed her the slow, stroking movements. "That's it!" as she imitated him.

Why, this isn't so hard, Amanda thought to herself. She became more daring and gradually eased away from Brady, eventually only holding on to his hand, the length of both their arms separating them. That's when she hit a bump in the ice and slipped, shrieking in surprise. Her fall was prevented by Brady's quick reflexes as he caught her and wrapped her in the safety of his strong arms.

"How kind of you to take me up on my offer to make a spectacle of yourself!" Brady grinned at her.

"Bradford Gallagher," she leaned away to sputter.

"I should never have told you my full name," he sighed ruefully. "You never fail to make use of it."

She felt his laughter rippling through her.

"You're too touchy!" Brady teased, his hands lending a new dimension to the adjective as they teased the nape of her neck before toying with her hair. "I like ruffling your feathers."

"I noticed."

"Did you now? I wasn't sure you would."

"Is that why you try so hard to drive me crazy, so I'll notice you?"

"Do I drive you crazy?" he inquired with feigned innocence.

"You know you do. Frequently," she added for good measure.

"Go on," he prompted. "This sounds like it could get interesting."

Amanda eyed him in exasperation. "You're impossible."

"Is that why I drive you crazy?"

"I'm not going to answer that," she refused. "What happened to my ice skating lessons?"

"They're temporarily on hold."

"So am I," she wryly noted. "Will you let me go now?"

"Not until you tell me why I drive you crazy."

"Brady, if you don't watch out, I'll tell your sister exactly how she can beat you at Monopoly."

"You wouldn't." One look at her face told him that she would. "Okay, okay. There, you're free." He released her from his embrace. "But I don't know what you're going to do with your freedom now that you've got it." This as Amanda struggled to stay upright and ended up clutched in Brady's arms again. "See what I mean."

"That's one of the reasons you drive me crazy."

"Oh?"

"You're always right!"

"How clever of you to notice," he modestly accepted.

"Oh, I can be very clever," she murmured, easing off her glove and running her hand along the angular curve of his jaw.

Brady lowered his head with deliberate slowness, an unconcealed hunger kindling in his eyes. Amanda's lips were parted and ready to receive his, their mouths meshing together with magical precision. Shooting sparks flickered behind Amanda's closed eyes while her heartbeat raced to get ahead. The need for oxygen finally made them pause.

Amanda huskily cautioned, "If you keep this up, the ice is going to melt and then we'll both end up in the drink!"

"You already go to my head like a potent drink," Brady husked in return. "And as for what you do to the rest of my anatomy . . ."

Amanda lifted a quick hand to stem the remainder of his sentence. "There are times, Brady, when words aren't necessary!" Her wicked contemplation of the unquestionably male contours of his body made him catch his breath. Since her hand was still pressed to his lips, Amanda could feel his abrupt inhalation and smiled knowingly. Brady didn't stay docile for long, however. He mouthed the cupped hollow of her bare palm, his tongue traveling across the basin. Excited by the erotic movement, Amanda was startled when his strong teeth softly nipped her thumb.

With an exaggerated "Ouch!" she immediately retrieved her hand.

"That was a reprimand from your instructor. Right now I'm supposed to be teaching you how to ice skate, but if you'd care to change the curriculum to a more intimate, indoor sport then that's fine with me. We should retire to a more suitable location though. A bedroom, perhaps?"

A grin threatened to ruin Amanda's deliberately shocked expression. "Detective Gallagher, what kind of woman do you take me for?"

"I'm trying to find out, but I don't seem to be getting very far," he complained.

When they were teasing each other like this it was hard to remember that an arsonist still plagued the college. But they were forced to remember the very next day, as yet another wastebasket fire was discovered. The students and staff members were in the midst of preparing for final exams, so the fire hazard turned an already hectic situation into something resembling bedlam.

It was a terrible week. Amanda spent several hours each day in staff meetings, devising ways to tighten library security and protect the college's irreplaceable collection of books. Brady sent an officer to counsel at one of the meetings, but was unable to attend himself due to his increased immersion in the investigation.

The library's computerized check-out system chose this week, one of the busiest times of the year, to break down, fraying already-spent nerves of students and employees alike. As soon as the computer system got back on line, three of the library's four coin-operated Xerox machines went on the fritz. Then there were the two library jobbers both vying for the college's juicy account. Amanda firmly put them both off; she had no intention of making a hurried decision she might later regret. With all this turmoil it was no surprise that Amanda looked forward to the weekend with more than usual anticipation.

Saturday morning was spent doing the wash and worrying about Brady. She knew he was putting in backbreaking hours at the station, not eating or resting properly. The few brief times she'd spoken to him on the phone this past week he'd sounded exhausted, almost discouraged.

Since Amanda planned on spending the day catching up on household chores, she dressed accordingly. Her jeans were bleached out from innumerable washings, and her flannel shirt was a baggy yet comfortable pick-up from the community hospital's resale shop. She padded around the house in bare feet, as she was apt to do when home alone. Her hair was seemingly haphazardly pinned on top of her head, several tendrils escaping their loose confinement.

A pair of lightweight headphones rested on her ears and the songs of Simon and Garfunkel filled her mind. These portable cassette players made housework much more bearable. The machine was small enough to hang from the belt loop of her jeans. She was singing her own soulful rendition of "Bridge over Troubled Waters" when the doorbell rang.

Amanda pulled the earphones down so they rested around her neck like a piece of technological jewelry. She wasn't expecting any company. Pausing to peek through the living room window, she saw Brady's Mustang parked out front. What was he doing here? And how could she answer the door dressed like an absolute grub? With a distracted hand, Amanda hurriedly attempted to tidy herself up while Brady rang the bell again.

"I'm coming," she yelled, shaking her head at the reflection she saw in the hall minor.

Brady looked exhausted, like he'd been up all night. His unshaven condition added to his haggard appearance. The sensuous shadow of the beginnings of a beard made his entire countenance seem darker.

"I'm sorry I didn't call . . ." he began before breaking off to demand, "What are you doing with my shirt?" His hand whipped out to tug on Amanda's flannel shirttail.

"Your shirt?" she repeated in confusion. "I don't have your shirt."

"Stop looking at me as if I were crazy," he wearily instructed. "I may be tired, but I'm not that tired. Where'd you get this shirt?"

"From the hospital resale shop. Why?"

"Because that's where my mother took my good luck shirt last spring. The moment I discovered it was missing I went to the resale shop to find it, but it had already been sold."

Amanda stared at him in amazement. "Are you trying to tell me that this shirt used to belong to you?"

"It always brought me luck, and God knows I sure as hell could use some right about now."

Amanda could feel Brady's banked frustration;

it was evident in the tenseness of his stance. Her voice was softly sympathetic as she murmured, "No luck on the investigation?"

"Nothing but a series of dead ends. I just can't seem to piece the clues together."

"You look beat. When was the last time you ate?"

"I don't know. Sometime last night."

"How about a roast beef sandwich with a bowl of hot soup?"

Brady wearily raked a hand through the dark curls of his hair. "Are you sure it's no trouble?"

"No trouble at all," she assured him. "I was going to take a lunch break anyway."

Amanda expected a teasing comment about her disheveled appearance, but Brady made none. In fact, he was unnaturally quiet. Amanda surreptitiously studied him while they ate their lunch. His face was all angles and shadows, the hooded slant of his eyes accentuated by exhaustion. Tired though he undoubtedly was, he still looked gorgeous. His hair seemed longer than it was the last time she'd seen him, curling down over his ears.

"Maybe you should go home and try to get some sleep," Amanda made the mistake of suggesting.

"How the hell am I supposed to sleep?" he exploded, "when at any moment some nut might set the whole damn college on fire!"

Amanda wasn't upset by his outburst; she realized his anger was self-directed. "Brady, you've got to get some rest. You're doing the best you can."

"Obviously my best isn't good enough!" Brady smashed his clenched fist on the table with a force that rattled their luncheon dishes. "Damn it, I'm missing something. There must be something, some clue that I'm overlooking. It's probably right there, staring me in the face, and I'm too blind to see it!"

He got up and started pacing across the room, hands jammed into his jeans pockets.

"There's only one thing that could blind you, Brady, and that's exhaustion. You really should try and get some rest."

"There's no point," he turned to mutter. "I wouldn't be able to sleep."

For just one fleeting moment the mask of male invincibility slipped and Amanda caught the vulnerability in Brady's eyes. It was enough to send her into his arms. They opened wide to receive her, closing around her with a fierceness that brought tears to her eyes. But they weren't tears of pain; they were a visible sign of how very moved she was.

Brady was no longer the great protector. Instead, he was the one who needed comfort, so she unstintingly gave it. Hugging him close, Amanda's loving embrace silently offered sympathy and support. Somehow their problems seemed halved when viewed from this magical circle.

There was no sexual implication in their actions,

no passionate excitement as experienced in their previous embraces. This was a time for a more basic universal need, the need for human understanding and consolation. Yet this, too, evoked emotion, a new kind of companionable warmth.

It could have been hours or minutes later when Brady finally eased away to say, “I’d like you to come with me.”

“Where are you going?”

“Someplace special. My place.”

“I thought you said you didn’t want to go home.”

“I didn’t say we were going to my home,” he corrected. “I said it was my place. You’ll see when we get there.”

Chapter Eight

Brady drove to the edge of town, crossing over the now frozen river. He stopped the car at a small pulloff and said, "We've got to walk the rest of the way."

Although it was only four in the afternoon, the sun was already preparing to set, its glowing rays mellowing the stark whiteness of the snow. "It's going to get dark soon," Amanda cautioned.

"I know, but it's not very far." He went around the car, opened the door for her, and held out his hand. "Are you coming?"

She twined her fingers through his. "Yes, I'm coming."

Fifteen minutes later they were standing on top of a bluff overlooking Deerfield. The same glaciers that had created the area's undulating landscape had also carved out the bluff they'd just ascended. "It's beautiful up here. Just like being in the . . ."

". . . mountains," Brady finished for Amanda. "In fact I used to call this my mountain, until I went to Garmisch and saw what real mountains are like."

"Have you been coming here long?" Amanda turned to ask.

"Since I was a kid."

"I never even knew this lookout was up here."

"Not many people do," Brady shrugged. "I prefer to keep it that way."

"You must've brought other people up here?"

"No. I told you this is my place. I've never shared it before."

"Why not?" She tried to catch his averted gaze.

"Because it never felt right."

"And now it does?"

He nodded, wrapping an arm around her shoulder. "It's peaceful up here, isn't it?"

"Very." Amanda graciously accepted the conversational shift. "It feels like we're on top of the world, far away from all the problems down there."

"I guess that's why I come up here. To get away from my problems."

"But you said you came here as a kid. Were you getting away from problems even then?"

Brady absently tugged her closer, his eyes focused on the distant horizon. "Even kids have problems, Mandy."

"I know," she sighed, recalling her own emotion-fraught adolescence.

"You speak as if from experience."

"Did I sound that bitter?" she laughed, somewhat self-consciously.

"You sounded . . ." He paused, searching for the right word. ". . . hurt. What happened?"

"It's a common enough story. My parents got divorced when I was thirteen. It was not an amicable separation. Things got very messy."

Brady shifted so that he was now slightly behind

her, his arms encircling her completely. "I'm sorry." He murmured the words against her ear.

Amanda relaxed against him, leaning her head back against his shoulder and letting the comfort of his embrace wash over her. "These things happen. You just have to learn from life's experiences and go on from there."

"And what did you learn from that experience?" he quietly asked.

Brady's question struck a nerve, a nerve too painful to probe. As she always did when backed into a corner, Amanda verbally side-stepped. "I learned that it's better to be in a position of asking the questions than answering them. Speaking of which, I've been meaning to ask you something."

"What?"

Her fingers slid down the material of his coat sleeve, until she reached his hand and the cool silver of his ID bracelet. "Who gave you this?"

Brady seemed surprised by her interest. "My parents. Why?"

She ignored his question, silently fingering the metal chain.

"Come on, Mandy." He tightened his arms with persuasive intent. "Why the interest?"

"All right," she spoke defiantly. "I thought an old girl friend might have given it to you."

"And that bothered you?" He smoothed back her hair, viewing her flushed profile with satisfaction. "Never mind, you don't have to answer that. I can see it bothered you."

"You don't have to sound so smug." The words

were meant to be a stern rebuke.

"Sorry," Brady grinned. "I'll work on that. And to think all this havoc was caused by a simple allergy to penicillin."

"Penicillin?" Her voice was laced with confusion. "I don't get the connection."

"That's why my parents gave me this bracelet. Turn it around," he instructed. "On the back side it lists the allergy."

Amanda lifted his left hand to read the engraved notice.

"It's because you're a cop, isn't it?" she concluded.

"That I'm allergic to penicillin? No, I don't think so."

"I meant the reason your parents gave you this bracelet. In case anything . . . happened to you in the line of duty."

"You make it sound like I'm on *Hill Street Blues*. Deerfield is comparatively quiet, aside from the current situation with the arsonist."

Which brought them right back to square one, the reason Brady had felt the need to get away for a while today.

"I'm sorry," Amanda apologized softly. "I didn't mean to bring that up."

"You didn't," he harshly denied. "It's me. I just can't seem to get a handle on this damn case!"

Amanda winced at the angry frustration his tone reflected. It hurt her to see him being so hard on himself. She wanted to help him, so she said,

"You're an excellent detective, Brady. Deerfield's police department is lucky to have you."

For some reason that was the wrong thing to say. She could feel his withdrawal even before he stepped away from her. She shivered suddenly, cold without his warmth beside her. "What's wrong?"

"Nothing's wrong." His assurance fell flat.

"Was it something I said?" she pressed.

But Brady maintained, "I'm fine."

"I can see you're not."

He ignored her concerned observation. "Come on, it's getting dark. We'd better get back to the car."

Brady walked ahead of her, his shoulders bent as though he were carrying the weight of the world upon them. Amanda caught up to him and walked beside him, her presence silently offering compassion. Then, unsure of his reaction, she slipped her arm across his back, conveying by touch the measure of her concern. Brady didn't reject her overture, instead his own arm came out to encircle her waist. A silent channel of communication existed between them, linking them together with nebulous chains.

When they were back in the car again, he turned to her and said, "Thanks." The grateful acknowledgment was accompanied by a tender flick to the tip of her nose.

"You're welcome. Maybe it would help if I gave you back your good luck shirt," Amanda offered.

She was pleased that her teasing suggestion elicited a laugh from Brady. "You'd give me the very shirt off your back?"

"I'd prefer not to at this very second. It is a little cold to be without a shirt."

"I could keep you warm," Brady leaned close to murmur seductively, stirring the tendrils of hair near her ear.

"Not in a car with bucket seats!" she cautioned.

"No problem. I planned ahead. This model doesn't have an in-the-floor console."

"You devious man!"

"Compliments will get you nowhere," he retorted. "Now do you want to get warmed up or not?"

"Yes, please."

"Then I'll turn on the heater," he mocked, his teasing eyes shining in the Mustang's shadowy interior.

"You don't need to do that," Amanda purred, reaching out a bold hand to lower the zipper on his winter jacket.

"I don't?" he echoed, watching her brazen fingers unbutton his shirt.

Amanda shook her head, slanting him an impudently saucy look. "You can supply all the warmth I need," she purred. While Brady was still recovering from the inviting provocation of her words, she placed her ice cold hands on the unprotected planes of his bare chest.

"You little devil!" he gasped.

"Compliments will get you nowhere," she recycled his words back to him.

"Then how about a little of this?" Brady reached for her, sliding her down onto the seat with one lithe, economical movement. His retributive hands pinned her to the vinyl upholstery in such a way that her bottom snugly filled the space between the two bucket seats. Her denim-clad legs tangled with his in the ensuing mirthful tousle.

"We're going to fog up your windows," she warned with a breathless laugh.

"You fog up my brain," Brady muttered, freeing the toggles of her stadium coat, unwrapping her like a present.

When he deftly unfastened her shirt, she had to tease him. "I guess this shirt must be yours. I always have trouble with those buttons!"

"Oh, Mandy!" he groaned. "I needed to see you today."

"You don't need to see all of me today," she gasped, stilling his hand on the waistband of her jeans.

Brady didn't protest her decision, resorting back to seductive humor. "It's too dark in here to see much of anything. I'll have to feel my way."

Amanda's breath caught in her throat as she felt his warm finger trail down the center of her body, from collarbone to navel. Since she wasn't wearing a bra, she'd expected a more aggressive approach, but Brady was a leisurely lover. His deliberately slow touch aroused her more than any urgent demand could ever have done. Her flesh actually tingled, as if he'd indelibly marked her with a kindling brand. Trembling perceptibly, she passionately chanted his name.

Brady lowered himself until the small space between them had disappeared entirely. Her hands tugged on his gapping shirt, freeing it from its imprisonment inside his jeans. She then gripped the bare flesh of his waist as he distributed his weight more evenly, taking care not to crush her.

With unhurried deliberation Brady's lips homed in on hers. Their kisses blended and incorporated the variety of emotions they were experiencing: desire, hunger, passion, and excitement. Brady's normally clean-shaven face was rough, but not enough to cause discomfort, just enough to add a new texture to his kisses.

Amanda's mouth molded itself to the shape of his, her tongue sampling his taste. It was a heady elixir she could easily get addicted to. She deeply inhaled the scent that was unique unto him, a combination of tangy shower soap and warm cotton shirts. She felt the pounding of his heart and heard the unsteadiness of his breathing.

True to his word, Brady did feel his way over her feminine curves, monitoring her palpable signs of arousal. Her gasp became a moan as his lips left the familiar softness of hers to wander across her collarbone before sinking lower, reconnoitering the creamy slopes of her breasts.

Amanda returned the favor, her lips mapping the slope of his shoulder and the underside of his jaw. Her slender fingers anchored themselves through the belt loops of his jeans while her thumbs swam across the sea of his bare skin.

As time went on, the aching need for fulfillment made itself more and more insistently known. Cocooned in a den of warmth, the interpretation of this as "making out on the front seat of a car" never entered her passion-hazed mind. Amanda was shivering under the onslaught of erotic sensations that were intoxicating her, and she communicated her desire by arching her body against his. She felt Brady's answering hardness and was amazed by his hidden power.

The syncopated sound of modern communication interrupted their passionate excursion.

"What's that?" Amanda hazily questioned

His voice was raspy with desire. "My beeper."

"Your what?"

But Brady was already moving away from her, automatically readjusting his clothing. "I've got to get to a phone and call headquarters."

"Headquarters?" Amanda knew her repetitive echoes sounded dense, but she couldn't help herself.

"I should've brought the unmarked squad car," he muttered to himself, turning the ignition on the Mustang. "Then I could've used the two-way radio."

Amanda was still trying to collect herself and the sides of her flapping shirt. As she'd complained, the buttons refused to cooperate for her. Overhearing her muffled curse, Brady turned to offer his assistance. "I'm sorry about this,

Mandy," he apologized while matching buttons to buttonholes. "But perhaps it's just as well, I'd hate the first time for us to be in the crowded confines of a car."

Amanda didn't know what to say to that. It seemed pretty useless to deny that that's where they'd been headed, not after the abandoned way she'd responded to him.

Brady stopped at the first gas station they came to, utilizing their pay phone. The leashed gait of his stride as he returned to the car warned her that something was up. "We've finally got a lead that's panned out. I'll drop you off at home, and then I've got to get back to the station."

Although she told herself not to, Amanda half-anticipated a call later from Brady, giving her some hint about what had happened on the case. There was no news until Monday afternoon. She was up to her elbows in reference tools, checking through issues of *Choice* magazine and selecting books. With over three thousand titles being published each month, the field had to be narrowed down considerably. Consequently numerous book reviews were used to justify each purchase.

Amanda prided herself on the library's evenly balanced collection. Too often librarians gave in to faculty pressure, as John did with Guy, and the results were a collection that didn't serve the students, but instead pampered certain professors' egos. It was a difficult compromise, with each department vying for their piece of the cake.

"Have you heard the news?" Beth burst into her office, shouting. "They caught the arsonist!"

Amanda removed her reading glasses. "You're kidding! How do you know?"

"I just talked to Carolyn, the switchboard operator. She said that the police came a few minutes ago and took some man with them — in handcuffs! And the dean's secretary told me that Dean Routledge will be issuing a memo within the hour to announce that the arsonist has been arrested. Officially they're withholding further information pending a decision on filing criminal charges."

Amanda knew from experience that official statements never affected the college grapevine. "Who was it?"

"Carolyn said it was one of the guys from Security."

Amanda was shocked. "From the college security force?"

"That's what she said."

"But why would he want to set fires around the campus?"

"I don't know. I guess you'll have to ask Brady."

Determined not to get into a discussion on Brady, Amanda vaguely replied, "I guess I will," before promptly returning to work. "Here is the first group of this month's book orders." She handed Beth a pile of neatly printed cards. "Remember to use our new jobber for all the general publishers."

Brady did finally call her, right before five,

with the promise that he'd stop by that evening. Amanda was told she'd have to wait until then for the details concerning the arrest. Brady arrived after dinner, just in time to sample the cinnamon cookies she was laying out on a cooling rack.

"So what happened?" Amanda eagerly prompted.

"Let me finish my cookie first," Brady protested. "You wouldn't want me talking while my mouth is full, would you?"

Since his statement had been mumbled around the cookie, she didn't see the difference. "You're already talking with your mouth full."

Brady was straddling one of her kitchen chairs, his folded arms resting on the top rung of the chair's back. "I'm sorry I didn't get back to you, but things started breaking pretty fast and there really wasn't time."

"That's all right," she allowed. "I did get a little worried though, when your mother said you didn't come home Sunday night."

"She told me you called." His look was one of warm approval.

"Did she warn you about fast older women?" Damn, what made her say that?

"Mandy!" He shook his head in exasperation. "You're not an older woman."

"I'm older than you are."

"Chronologically, perhaps. As I've told you before, you worry too much about appearances."

"How did we get onto this subject?" she interrupted, as she always did when he got too close to the truth. "You were going to tell me about the arsonist."

"I suppose you've already heard that it was someone from college security."

Amanda nodded. "The campus grapevine is very efficient."

"I know," Brady acknowledged. "That was one of the reasons it took us so long to catch this guy. He always seemed to be one step ahead of us."

"Do you know why he set the fires?"

"Via the same college grapevine, he'd heard that several of the Security positions were going to be downgraded to part-time status. Setting the fires was his way of assuring himself job security."

"Didn't he realize that any one of those fires could have seriously injured, even killed people?"

"He was desperate, and desperation doesn't lend itself to contemplation."

Amanda turned to look at Brady in surprise. He shifted in his seat, tugging his hair in a gesture she'd come to know as a sign of embarrassment.

His self-observation was deliberately wry. "Pretty heavy philosophy for a small-town cop, right?"

"Left," she teased.

"I'm never going to hear the end of that, am I?"

"I still haven't heard how you caught the arsonist. What made you suspect him?" Her voice reflected her enthusiasm as she asked, "Did you identify his fingerprints, or did you trace the matches that started the fire?"

"I can tell you're a mystery buff," Brady sighed. "I'm sorry there was nothing spectacular, no singular clue. It was a combination of a number of things that, when pieced together, pointed to someone within the security force itself. A motivational study provided the rest."

The lack of a single case-cracking clue didn't upset her. "Maybe now we can all concentrate on the upcoming Christmas holiday."

"Only twenty more shopping days," Brady recited. "So when are you going to get a tree?"

"I don't know." Amanda stole a cookie for herself. "I haven't thought about it yet."

"You're not going to tell me that you're too old to celebrate Christmas, are you?" His inflection warned her that she'd be in trouble if she tried it.

"No, I wasn't going to say that," Amanda denied. "I made these cookies for the holiday."

Brady's face fell with boyish disappointment. "I thought you made them for me."

"At the rate you're eating them, there won't be any left by tomorrow, let alone Christmas."

"You'll just have to bake some more, won't you," was his practical suggestion.

"Slavedriver!"

"If I were a slavedriver, I'd make you chop down your own tree instead of offering to do it for you."

"I haven't heard you offer to do it for me," she pointed out.

"I just did. When are you free?"
"I'm never free," she murmured seductively. "But for you I could be reasonable."
"Name your price," was his intimate invitation. He waited for the telltale signs of a blush before adding, "I was talking about the tree, of course."
"Of course," Amanda murmured, cursing her fair complexion.
They set off after work on Friday to one of the nearby nurseries that grew Christmas trees. Brady chose a hearty balsam and started chopping. His selection of holiday jokes had Amanda in stitches, tears of mirth running down her cold cheeks.
"Are you sure this doesn't hurt the tree?" she was teasing when Brady suddenly cursed under his breath, his stroking chops abruptly ceasing.
"I think it just hurt me a hell of a lot more than I hurt the damn tree!" he swore.
"What did you do?" Amanda breathed in fear, visions of a disastrous accident filling her with dread.
"This damn tree obviously wasn't meant to be cut down by a southpaw." Brady held out his badly scraped left hand. "That lower branch got closer than I thought."
Amanda cradled his injured hand to her cheek, unmindful of the tears still streaking her face.
The salty wetness was enough to bring a grimace of pain to Brady's face. "Honey, you're rubbing salt in my wounds!"
"I'm sorry," she apologized, quickly lowering

his hand from her face, but still retaining it in her cautious clasp. "How can I make it better?"

"You could try seducing me," he judiciously decided.

"And deprive you of the chase?" she countered with a choked laugh. "I wouldn't dream of it."

"Well, I sure as hell do," he growled. "Frequently!"

Amanda was unable to hide the reciprocal awareness that his husky admission evoked. It was reflected in the responsive softness of her eyes, the tremor of her fingers. She held his gaze as long as she could, the pagan message in their depths depriving her of air and forcing her to break the visual tug of war. Her eyes fell on the strong masculine hand she still held. The damage to his knuckles was probably painful, but not serious. "You've got a very wide hand." She murmured her thought aloud.

"The better to hold you with, my dear," Brady chortled in the voice of a wicked wolf.

"But apparently not the better to chop down trees with."

Brady dramatically clutched his chest, drawing her hand up with his. "Only a cruel woman would hit a man when he's down."

"That's the problem, you see," Amanda humorously explained, enjoying herself tremendously. "The tree's the one that's supposed to be going down, not you."

Brady released her hand, imperiously waving her away. "Stand aside, woman, and let me finish my quarrel with this mighty giant!"

Amanda refused to budge. "Not until I bandage your wounds from the last quarrel!" She removed a spotless handkerchief from her shoulder bag. "I always knew that this would come in handy someday. Did I hurt you?" she asked in response to Brady's groan.

"No, that groan was entirely due to your pun," he explained, referring to her use of the word *handy*.

"It was an unintentional one, I assure you," she retorted, efficiently binding up his hand.

They got the tree into Amanda's living room without further difficulty, although there was a tricky moment when it appeared that the evergreen was going to get stuck, trapping Brady between it and the door frame. Amanda had laughingly told Brady that if he'd eaten any more of her cookies, he wouldn't have fit through.

When the tree was completely decorated, Amanda switched off the room lights and plugged in the string of colored bulbs nestled in the fragrant pine branches.

"Where'd you get so many ornaments?"

"I collect them," Amanda admitted.

Brady looked interested. "From when you were a kid?"

"No," she answered abruptly. "We moved around too much to keep track of things like ornaments."

"I thought you said you were born in Deerfield."

"I was, in this very house as a matter of fact."

"You never told me that before."

"It never came up," she shrugged. "Anyway, we moved when I was about nine or ten. My father got a job at a university back east. We moved twice over the next few years, and then of course there was the divorce. My mom ended up in California; my father is in Virginia, I believe."

Brady picked up on that immediately. "You believe?"

"We're not that close." Her tone didn't invite persual of the subject.

"How did you manage to regain possession of 'your' house?"

"It went on the market shortly after I returned to Deerfield."

"I see," he murmured, even though he didn't quite. "You're very protective about your past, aren't you?"

"So are you."

"What do you want to know?" Brady invited, resting comfortably on her couch. He wore a checked cotton shirt with his jeans, as usual. While they may not have been fashionable designer attire, the working denims fit him to a T.

"A lot of things. What you did after the army, what you said to Guy Lox?" Amanda was pleased with the smooth way she inserted that into the conversation.

"Lox? Why bring him up?"

"Because I heard the two of you had a little

meeting in his office this week."

"The college grapevine again," he sighed, before stating hopefully, "I don't suppose you'd believe we were just having a little chat."

Amanda shook her head.

"I didn't think so. Okay, we talked about you."

"Me? Why?"

"Because of the little incident during the last faculty wine and cheese party. You didn't think I guessed about his behavior, did you."

"Brady, Professor Lox is on the faculty library committee. I hope you didn't . . ." She paused, struggling for the right way to word it.

"Smash his face in and threaten to break his arms," Brady obligingly filled in.

"Did you?"

"No. I can't say I wasn't tempted though."

"Then what *did* you say?"

"Simply that for his future well-being he'd better stop harassing the woman I love."

"You told him that!" she croaked, her heart lodged in her throat.

"Sure did," Brady answered cheerfully enough. "And now I'm telling you." His voice softened magically, its inflection winding its way around her heart. "I love you, Mandy."

Chapter Nine

Amanda stared at Brady's face, unable to believe her ears. Had he really said he loved her? Just like that? No wine, no flowers, no music? No warning!

"Maybe you'd better sit down," he ruefully suggested. "I surprised you, huh?"

Amanda could only nod.

"Didn't you guess?" he prompted with affectionate exasperation. "Couldn't you tell how I felt about you?"

"I knew you wanted to make love to me, that you were attracted to me; but I didn't think about love."

"Well, start thinking about it!" His teasing manner hid his uncertainty.

"I don't know w-what to say," Amanda stuttered.

"I can see that. It's all right," he soothed, getting up to stand beside her. "You don't have to say anything."

Amanda didn't know who initiated the embrace, and she didn't care as long as she was close to him. The familiar rush of pleasure she experienced whenever he was near made her stop and consider. The pleasure, the passion, the desire, she felt at the look, feel, and taste of him; could this be love? Or was it a dangerous facsimile?

"Since I've gone this far, I might as well go the rest of the way," Brady murmured against the top of her head. Taking a deep breath, he stepped back and cupped her face with his hands, his gaze direct and unwavering. "I'd like us to go away together for a weekend, away from interrupting beepers and distracting phone calls. We need to talk."

"Just talk?"

His dark eyes were warm with loving intent while his voice tenderly wooed her. "No, not just talk. I want to make love to you, and I want it to be slow and perfect. I know of a country inn a few hours from here. They boast that there's a fireplace in every room. Will you come with me?"

A rush of relief welled over her. He wasn't talking about marriage, he was talking about an affair. A love affair, granted, but nothing legally binding. He understood, as he always seemed to understand her, without words, without explanations. "Yes, Brady. I'll come with you."

"I've booked us for the weekend before Christmas."

"You were that sure of me?" she huffed, trying to look suitably indignant when all she could really think about was the intimate promise of an entire weekend spent in Brady's arms.

"I'm not sure of you at all," was Brady's husky admission.

Amanda nuzzled closer, her thoughts dreamy.

She didn't speak, for words got in the way. Instead she enjoyed the moment for what it was, with the added piquancy of knowing that in a matter of a few days they would be forging yet another link. Their relationship had never been a mad rush, it had evolved over the time they'd known each other, and each step was a natural progression. That fact made her feel certain that her decision to go away with Brady was the right one.

Amanda planned her wardrobe with more than usual care. She chose outfits that were designed with sexy frivolity in mind, a far cry from her usual tailored cautiousness. Even her undies were pale clouds of sheer delight!

Friday after work she rushed home to soak in a bubble bath, pinning her freshly set hair out of the way. While rubbing on a fragrant body lotion, she speculated about Brady's reaction to its sensuous scent. Her wool skirt was a deceptively simple wraparound in muted tones of beiges and browns. A matching vest covered her tawny blouse. She kept her makeup deliberately light, the neutral tones highlighting her features.

Despite all this preparation, Amanda was still nervous, and it showed in her unnatural quietness once they were on their way.

"What are you thinking about?" Brady queried, noting the small smile curving her lips.

"You," she answered honestly.

Brady's lips now sported a matching smile. "What about me?"

"I was thinking about the way you hold a phone."

"The way I hold a phone?" he repeated in bewilderment.

"You did ask."

"I know I did, but I don't know why you were thinking about the way I hold a phone."

"It's not as crazy as it sounds," she began.

"Well, that's reassuring," Brady inserted, his smile progressing to a grin.

"I was thinking of all the things I like about you," she explained, "and that was one of them."

"You like the way I hold a phone?" He was incredulous.

"Will you stop saying it like that?"

"I'm sorry, but I don't see what there is to like or dislike about holding a phone."

"That's because you've never paid any attention to it. Some people grasp the center of the receiver as if it were a dumbbell, but you cradle the mouthpiece in your hand, bracing it against the heel of your palm."

"And what does that tell you about me?" Brady's question rode on a ripple of laughter.

"I don't know. It's just one of those idle observations."

"Don't tell me, let me guess. You read about it in one of your mysteries."

"I did not," she denied. "I was thinking about your quirks."

"I'd rather you thought about my . . ."

"Don't say it," she warned.

"How can you tell what I was going to say?"

"It was written all over your face."

"And you can read in the dark?"

"Mmm," she affirmed. "Didn't know that, huh?"

"No. Do now though. I'll have to be more deviously mysterious."

"Now I see why Wisconsin is nicknamed the badger state. They named it after you."

"I've never badgered you," he immediately denied.

Amanda's tone was one of mocking disbelief. "No?"

He had the grace to look a little shamefaced. "Well, maybe a tiny bit. But you deserved it."

"I did? Why, what did I ever do?"

"You sicced that beefy security officer on me the first time we met."

"We hadn't actually met when I *sicced* him on you," she corrected. "I didn't know who you were. Besides, I apologized for that."

"In a very unsorry voice."

"I wasn't used to frisking cops," she defended herself.

"And I wasn't used to librarians who frisked."

"Did you tell your mother where you were spending the weekend?" Amanda switched the subject by asking.

"Why?" Brady countered. "Do I need a note of permission?"

"No. It's just that I know how close you are

to your family and I wondered what you told them."

"That I would be unavailable until Monday."

"That's all?"

"That's all. My family respects my privacy."

"It must be nice."

"What must be nice?"

"Having a family that's there when you need them, and not when you don't."

"Speaking of being there, I think that's the turnoff for the Stonehearth Inn coming up." Brady proficiently eased the Mustang onto the cleared expanse of the narrow drive. "Here we are. What do you think of it?"

Amanda squinted through the snow-speckled windshield. "It looks lovely."

As its name implied, the building was made of natural stone. Falling flakes of snow were silhouetted against the lighted windows. Brady hauled both their pieces of luggage out of the car's trunk and motioned Amanda ahead of him. A large Christmas tree and a roaring fire gave the small lobby an immediate sense of cheer. Their landlord was polite and discreet, making Amanda wonder if Brady had been here before.

Their weekend package came with a candlelit dinner served in their room — roast duckling with sage stuffing, wild rice, and tiny peas. Afterward they sat in front of their promised fireplace to savor the last toasts of champagne. They'd both taken off their boots and left them on the mat by the door. Artificial illumination would have dispelled the room's romantic ambience, so the light switches were all left in the off position.

The amber firelight played over the nylon-covered length of Amanda's legs, drawing Brady's attention to their slim perfection. Removing the half-empty champagne glass from her hand, he drew her back to recline against him, her back resting on his chest. His arms crossed over in front of her, the firm muscles of his forearms brushing the soft curvaceousness of her breasts. Amanda relaxed against him, at home in the warmth of his embrace. Their voices were low and soft as they reminisced about the past.

Brady began with, "What did you think when you first met me?"

"That you were toying with me," Amanda eventually admitted.

Brady had to smile at her quaint terminology. "No way. I will confess to wanting to play with you though. With your hair, with your lips, with your body."

"Is that all you wanted?" she questioned provocatively.

"No," he leaned away to recollect with a grin. "I also wanted to tease you off your pedestal."

"Was I on a pedestal?" She sneaked a finger in between the buttons of his blue shirt, lightly running her nail across his unprotected skin.

"You were when I first met you, but you're not now. Now you're driving me to distraction." He caught her taunting finger and lazily nipped at it with his even, white teeth.

"The Distracted Detective," she mused, moving her hand out of harm's way to play with his dark curls. "That sounds like a title of one of my mysteries."

"I think it's about time I unraveled a little of your mystery," he decided, slipping off the woolen vest she was wearing.

"You know, when I was at the police academy I was always getting in trouble for not doing things by the book," he conversationally imparted, tossing her vest over the back of the couch.

"Does that mean you believe in creative investigating?" she quipped with an anticipatory smile.

"Definitely. Shall I give you a free demonstration?" he generously offered.

"Please do!"

He slid her onto his lap, bending his legs and tumbling her onto his chest, whereupon he began softly blowing in her ear. Amanda automatically giggled, expecting the gentle tickling to evoke laughter. But it didn't, it evoked another emotion entirely, one that raised goosebumps up and down the length of her arm. Meanwhile his hands were busy, faithfully practicing the art of creative investigating. She'd never encountered a man with such a developed sense of touch, and he used it as a means of sharing rather than as a brand of possession.

Amanda's finger investigated the slant of his eyebrows with a newly discovered sense of possession. "You have such wide brows," she marveled.

"To match my wide hands," which he used to give her such pleasure that it shuddered down her spine.

"And beautiful lips." Amanda's index finger lovingly outlined the catalogued item.

Brady looked at her as if he wanted to inhale her and keep her within him forever. The passionate intensity of his gaze seared her, setting alight an answering flame deep within her. This was it. They retired to the bed, prepared to embark on a sensual exploration that would lead them into the incandescent pleasures of love.

Brady's shirt was the first deposit on what was to become a steadily increasing pile of clothing. Amanda's fingers skied down the angled slope of his shoulders, refamiliarizing herself with the welcoming terrain of his powerful body. He was a study of warm flesh and rippling muscles; there wasn't an ounce of surplus fat anywhere. Amanda explored the central valley down his chest, tracing its origins to the flat planes of his stomach. Her fingers boldly lowered to trace the carved surface of his belt buckle.

"Wait," Brady murmured, catching her hand and returning it to his bare chest. "It's my turn." The ingenious fastenings of her blouse were opened quickly and the garment fell open. He caught his breath as the sizzling filminess of her lingerie was revealed to him for the first time.

The dusky rosiness of her nipples glowed

through the sheer shine of the material cupping them, beckoning his lavish attention. She shivered and burned as his fingertips skimmed their surface. His head bent to administer the next divine caress, his curls dark against her paleness. The long hypnotic strokes of his tongue permeated the diaphanous covering until she was aflame with desire.

Realizing that her blouse had now joined his shirt on the floor, Amanda resumed her tinkering with his belt buckle. There seemed something almost hedonistically wicked about the measured slowness of their pace. Brady was just beginning on the intricacies of her skirt when she finally undid his belt buckle and unsnapped the riveted fastener.

"I told you that you'd be good at this." Brady's husky words of encouragement were murmured somewhere near her temple.

Amanda shook her head in wonder. "I never knew . . ."

"You'll find out tonight," he promised, tossing her wraparound skirt to the floor.

Brady was delighted to discover that the taupe nylon encasing her legs was held up by a sexy garter belt instead of proletarian panty hose. Propping himself up on one elbow, he drank in the picture of seductiveness she made. The silky material of her camisole matched that of her French panties. Her honey-gold hair tumbled over her shoulders, its glorious disarray caused by the combing caresses of his hands. Her eyes were sable-dark with impassioned desire, her look one of sensual arousal. Brady had never seen anything as beautiful, and he said so as his hand reached out to trace spiraling patterns on the sensitive crook of her knee.

"You've given new meaning to the phrase 'sheer delight.' " The husky stroke of his voice was a caress in itself.

"I wore these for you."

"They're great. You're great." His "great" was a heady distillation of all the compliments she'd ever been given, a thousand times more potent than the strongest wine.

Brady released her stockings from their holders, the warmth of his fingers evocatively brushing against the delicate skin of her inner thighs. As soon as her stockings were dispensed with, Amanda tugged Brady back down beside her so that she could ease open the zipper of his jeans, working the denim covering off his hips, down his legs, and out of the way.

Sexy though her lingerie may have been, it was still a barrier not to be borne. The camisole top was stroked away first, having fulfilled its mission of amplifying the delicacy of his touch. Now, without that barrier, the stimulation was purely concentrated. His hands began the manipulations, followed by the magic of his mouth and flicking tongue until the ripe fullness blossomed with complete arousal. Rose peaks strained against his hand, their taut hardness fascinating him.

Her wide-legged French panties were saved

until last. They were more an enticement than a deterrent, their unconstricted design allowing for innumerable forays under their protection.

Amanda's voice was heavy with desire as she whispered, "That feels so . . ."

"How do I make you feel?" Brady murmured.

"Like all the bones in my body have melted and turned into warm gelatin with an ache . . ."

"Where? Here?"

"Mmm," she purred, rhythmically rubbing against the hand that stroked the treasure trove of her femininity.

Hurtling through space had never appealed to Amanda, yet she welcomed the sensation with Brady. He set her humming until every pulsating outpost of her body was clamoring for release. Now nothing separated them, bare skin clung to bare skin. Her body yearned to accommodate his, yet still he held back, helping her realize her true potential.

Like a liberated tigress, Amanda raked her nails across the rippling expanse of his back, demanding satisfaction. Brady anchored her writhing body with his while she absorbed him into her very being. Flares of passion overcame her consciousness, blacking out everything but the life-giving current that flowed between them.

Afterward, her head lay pillowed on his shoulder, her limbs entangled with his as she physically expressed her desire to remain close to the warm male body that had supplied so much pleasure.

It was some time before they'd recovered sufficient breath to speak in more than incoherent rushes.

"You're great," Amanda murmured against the salty bareness of his skin.

"So are you," he whispered, threading a tender hand through her hair.

Both voices reflected their wonder. In the twilight of early morning they made love again, and again it was slow and exquisitely sensuous.

It was midmorning before the two closely entwined figures in the double bed showed signs of awakening. Amanda was the first one up, tugging on a powder blue robe she had to recover from her still unpacked suitcase.

"It's a crime to cover that body with a robe," Brady's sleepy voice informed her from the bed.

"It's a crime to leave it uncovered," she archly countered, firmly tying the belt. "Ever heard of indecent exposure?"

"There isn't one inch of that body that's indecent. I know, I've surveyed it all!"

Amanda giggled at his roguishly leering expression.

"Come back to bed, woman," Brady growled. "I want to talk to you."

"A likely story," she tossed over her shoulder, deliberately heading in the opposite direction.

Brady grabbed her and in an instant had her pinned to the tousled bedclothes. "Gottcha!"

"Your behavior is most ungentlemanly, Detective Gallagher," she reprimanded.

"And your behavior last night was most unladylike." He watched her blush with fascination. "Most unladylike," he repeated, "but most enjoyable!" He lifted one of the hands he'd held captive and studied the polished ovals of her fingernails. "How'd you get such long nails?"

"I eat tacks for breakfast," she pertly quipped.

Brady grinned. "That must be why you're so tough."

No, she could have replied, *that took years of practice.* She could have made such a reply, but didn't because her background wasn't a subject she cared to discuss.

"I'd like to talk about my intentions," Brady solemnly stated.

"Which I'm sure are wickedly dishonorable," she teased, her fingers tiptoeing across his bare chest.

"You're not making this easy for me," he muttered thickly. "I'm talking about marriage. Between you and me. Hell, I'm not doing this very well!" His features wore an expression of masculine discomfiture. "I'm trying to ask you to marry me, Mandy. Will you?"

Amanda's eyes widened in dismay.

"I know you haven't actually come out and said that you love me," Brady continued, "but I know you wouldn't have agreed to come away with me this weekend if you didn't. I guess the words must be hard for you to say. I can understand that. They're not that easy for me either. But I do love you, Mandy, and I want to marry you."

He gazed down at her expectantly. Gradually the inappropriateness of her expression sank in. "What's wrong? You look like I just kicked you instead of proposing."

His description was accurate; that's exactly how she felt, as though she'd been kicked in the stomach. All this time she'd been sure that Brady understood her, that she was safe with him. Now it turned out that he didn't understand at all, or he would never have even mentioned marriage.

"I'm not ready for marriage," was her cool refusal.

"Not ready!" Brady repeated in exasperation. "Mandy, you're thirty years old." He knew the words were a mistake the moment he spoke them. He was right. He could feel her leaving him, withdrawing into herself and erecting her defensive shields. "Mandy, I didn't mean that the way it sounded."

But she ruthlessly cut off his denial. "Of course you did. As a thirty-year-old spinster librarian I should be ecstatic over a proposal of marriage. But I'm not ecstatic."

"I can see that." His voice was very quiet. "Don't you love me?"

"It isn't a matter of loving you," she wearily declared.

"Then what is it a matter of?" he questioned in impatient confusion.

"It's a matter of marriage."

He drew in a deep breath, the nerve jumping

along his jaw a visible sign of turbulent emotions held in check. "Marriage with me?"

"You have nothing to do with it."

Brady flinched as though stuck. "I see," he grated. Amanda was instantly freed. Rolling off the bed, he grabbed for his jeans, closing the zipper and fastening the snap with angry, jerky movements. This time when his voice burned her, it was with anger. "You'll have to forgive me if I've been a little slow. I haven't had the years of schooling that you've had and am not accustomed to these psychological games."

Amanda looked at him in bewilderment, wishing she'd been better prepared for this eventuality. "I'm not playing games, Brady."

"Aren't you?" Clearly he didn't believe a word. "I'd call this whole thing a game, a charade. You came away with me this weekend for a quick thrill, a little pre-holiday excitement. After all, you're a liberated woman. It's perfectly all right to sleep with someone like me, so long as you don't marry them!"

Amanda was horrified at his conclusions. "Brady, I didn't plan it like this. I had no idea you were thinking of marriage!"

But he wasn't listening. "God, I should've seen it sooner," he berated himself. "You were forever avoiding your friends when we were together. You got furious when I implied we had a relationship in front of them."

"Why do you have to take this so personally?" she cried.

"Meaning any man would've done?" he lashed out.

"No, I don't mean that." The flush on her cheeks was now caused by equal parts of anger and embarrassment. "I don't sleep around!"

"You weren't a virgin," he starkly stated.

"Neither were you!" she shot back, angered by this display of the old double-standard. Her previous sexual experience had been limited to one fling while she was at college, and Brady had no right slinging accusations about her moral standards.

Brady, however, had no way of knowing that her experience was limited. "Well, I'm sorry to shatter your dreams, but I don't intend to provide stud service for you! I don't like being used, lady!" His face was set in grim lines, all traces of boyish humor erased.

"I never meant to use you," she fiercely denied.

"Really?" His inflection was one of scornful disbelief.

"Yes, really."

"Get dressed," he commanded in a flat tone. "We're going back to Deerfield."

Amanda wrapped the robe around her shivering form and got up off the bed. While gathering her suitcase she turned to steal a look at Brady, but his rigid back was turned to her, his fierce pride up in arms.

Once in the bathroom, anger carried her through the difficult task of putting on another matched set of lingerie similar to the ones Brady had stroked away only hours before. It wasn't her fault that their romantic weekend had turned into a disaster. Brady was the one who'd ruined everything by bringing up marriage. Why couldn't he have left well enough alone?

The flirtatiousness of her attire mocked her, making Amanda angrily button her blouse up to the collar. There, that was better. Now even her wraparound skirt seemed more tailored. She opened the bathroom door to find Brady already packed and obviously eager to leave.

She felt it only fair that she be given a chance to defend herself. "I never meant to lead you on."

"You'll have to forgive me if I find that hard to believe," was his savagely sarcastic retort.

"I'm sorry," she apologized with haughty dignity.

"And I don't buy that either."

Brady headed out the door, leaving Amanda to follow with her suitcase in hand, feeling very much like a recalcitrant schoolgirl instead of a mature woman in charge of her life.

Their drive home was nerve-racking. It was snowing steadily and the roads were rapidly becoming a sheet of ice. Amanda stayed silent, leaving Brady to concentrate on his driving. The obdurate line of his jaw warned of his tightly leashed anger.

When they finally pulled up in front of her house, she let herself out of the claustrophobic confines of the Mustang. Brady retrieved her things from the trunk and handed it to her, studiously avoiding even the slightest physical contact. Huge flakes of snow nestled in his curly hair, their coldness matching the icy bleakness in his eyes. His farewell was equally glacial.

"Good-bye, Amanda. It's been most educational."

She'd been dismissed.

Chapter Ten

It was one of the worst Christmases Amanda could ever remember enduring. She resented all the happy festivity, the smiling faces, the general good will. Her brusque manner at work had elicited worried glances at first, but as Amanda ruthlessly dispatched all attempts at sympathy, those glances became jaundiced. The library staff's hopes that she would resume her normal equanimity after the week-long Christmas break were shattered on the first day back. Amanda was even worse than before. That's when Beth finally took it upon herself to lodge a protest.

"Look, I know that in your present mood I could lose my job over this, but somebody's got to talk to you, Amanda."

They were in Amanda's office, and both doors were closed to shut out curious eavesdroppers. "About what?" Amanda impatiently demanded, not bothering to look up from the report she was compiling.

"About the way you've been acting. What's happened, Amanda? Was it something between you and Brady?"

Amanda's already cool expression immediately frosted. "Beth, I realize we're friends, but that doesn't give you the right to discuss private matters during business hours."

"They're not private matters when they interfere with work," Beth was forced to point out.

"Are you implying that I'm letting personal problems affect my work?" Amanda icily inquired.

Many would have been intimidated and given up, but Beth was genuinely concerned about the change in her friend's behavior and she refused to back down. "Amanda, please talk to me. Tell me what's wrong."

Amanda wearily shoved her hair away from her face. "All right," she finally sighed, "but I can't talk about it here. If you're free tonight, maybe we could go out to dinner and discuss it."

They ate at a restaurant near the campus. Amanda ordered a chef's salad, which she only picked at.

Beth voiced her concern. "I'm worried about you."

"Don't be. I'm fine."

"Sure. And I'm Bo Derek," she retorted. "Come on, Amanda, what is it?"

Amanda absently crumbled a dinner roll with the back of her fingernail as she replied, "It was Brady, indirectly."

"Indirectly?"

"We're no longer seeing each other." Amanda's voice was deliberately matter-of-fact. "The entire thing was a mistake from the first. I should've known better."

"Wasn't he serious about you?"

"Too serious," she bitterly retorted.

Beth was clearly puzzled. "How can you be too serious?"

"He wanted marriage," was Amanda's flat response.

"So?"

"I didn't."

"Why not?"

Amanda shifted uncomfortably in her seat. "I didn't want it."

"Why not?" Beth repeated. "You're obviously in love with him."

"I am not," Amanda heatedly denied with more emotion than she'd shown in a long time. "I can't love indiscriminately. I want to be discriminating in my emotions."

"What you want and what you get are two different things. What's wrong with being in love with Brady?"

"It wouldn't work."

"What wouldn't work?"

"Marriage."

"Why not?"

"Because the odds are bad enough when two people have a lot in common."

"You mean come from the same background," Beth interpreted. "Are you ashamed of Brady?"

"No. I'm just being sensible. I mean, look at the facts. He's a down-to-earth cop who likes beer and baseball."

"From what you told me he also likes strawberry-rhubarb pie and classical music."

"He's stubborn."

"He's independent," Beth substituted. "Lefties are like that. Because they've encountered so many challenges to their competence and autonomy, they end up preferring to figure out problems for themselves."

"Where did you hear that?"

Beth smiled. "I checked out the same book you did!"

Amanda avoided her friend's knowing look, but Beth didn't let up. "Amanda, he's a great guy. He can be considerate and sensitive without having those characteristics in any way detract from his masculine sureness or strength. And while he may not be fancy, he is honest and straightforward."

Part of Amanda acknowledged that all Beth's accolades were true, but another part stubbornly questioned the practicality of their relationship. "It just wouldn't work."

"If you're so sure it wouldn't work, why are you so miserable?"

"I'm not miserable."

"You've been reenacting the Reign of Terror at the library. The staff is afraid to even breathe for fear of setting you off!"

"I'm sorry if you think that I've been unusually harsh. You know John is retiring next month and I desperately want the position of head librarian. I've got to whip the place into shape before then, to show the administration what I can do."

"That all sounds very convincing, but I don't believe a word of it."

Amanda refused to be drawn out and Beth was forced to give up. While she didn't condone Amanda's behavior, at least now she understood the reasons for it, even if Amanda herself didn't.

Talking to Beth hadn't helped the situation. At work the next day Amanda was even more short-tempered. Her patience was practically nonexistent, her temper icily volatile.

When Amanda saw Helen working on the same booktruck full of new acquisitions for the second day in a row, her temper flared. "Helen, why isn't this material out on the shelves yet? It's of no use to the students if you're going to hide it back here in Technical Services. We're not ordering these things for our own entertainment and use," she said sharply.

Helen's face reddened under the scornful inflection of Amanda's chilly voice, but she remained silent.

"I don't know how you have your task priorities listed, but getting new material out on the shelves is supposed to be on the top. See that this booktruck is shelved before the end of the day!" Amanda ordered with brusque efficiency.

Her reprimand delivered, Amanda pivoted and returned to her own office. Twinges of guilt were quick to make themselves felt, and she meant to get back to Helen and apologize for being so rough on her. But several vendor problems arose, long-distance calls that demanded her immediate attention and temporarily postponed her apology. It was a little after four before she got the time to search Helen out. Beth told her that the older woman was shelving in the stacks.

Amanda saw the booktruck before she saw Helen. It was jutting out from one of the last aisles. As she got closer she saw that Helen was struggling to rearrange an entire unit, shifting books in order to fit in the new materials.

Amanda was just about to make her presence known when the older woman sat back from her squatting position and just seemed to keel over, clutching her throat. The carpeting protected Helen from severe injury after the fall, but Amanda didn't have time to worry about that.

Automatically reaching for Helen's pulse, she noted its feeble unevenness in dismay. When Helen suddenly stopped breathing, Amanda knew what she had to do. Shouting out for help, she immediately began administering cardiopulmonary resuscitation. She'd taken the lessons from the local Red Cross two years before, but had never before been called upon to use the lifesaving technique. Her arms were soon aching from the fatiguing exertion, but she didn't falter. Two students had come running to her aid, but neither of them were familiar with CPR and were unable to assist other than to call an ambulance.

Amanda had no knowledge of how long she worked on Helen before the paramedics arrived. All she knew was that the older woman had resumed breathing, but it was still dangerously shallow. Helen was whisked away on a stretcher while a benumbed Amanda provided information about Helen's family's names and phone numbers.

Beth walked up and put her arm around Amanda, guiding her away from the attendant crowd that had gathered. John Abbington pompously pushed his way to the fringe of the assemblage, halting the women's progress with his words.

"It's incredibly bad management, Amanda, to work your employees until they literally drop!"

"It wasn't Amanda's fault," Beth immediately defended, appalled at the head librarian's insensitivity.

"I never said it was," John fastidiously corrected, his bald head shining. "I was merely pointing out that I happened to overhear Amanda's earlier confrontation with this assistant and thought it most unprofessional."

"I've got to go to the hospital," Amanda blankly stated. John was right, of course. Helen's attack was her fault, all her fault. She should never have yelled at the older woman like that, should never have pushed her to get those books shelved.

"Let me drive you," Beth offered.

Amanda shook her head. "I'll be fine."

Beth had misgivings, but Amanda was adamant. Concerned all the same, Beth called the hospital a short while later and asked about Helen's condition. There was no news. When she inquired if Amanda was still waiting, the nurse told her that Miss Richards had left shortly after arriving.

When Beth dialed Amanda's home number there was no reply. She even drove by and banged on the front door, but Amanda's Porsche wasn't in the driveway or in the garage. After four hours had passed, still without any word from Amanda, Beth became desperate and phoned Brady at the police station. Perhaps he'd know where to look for Amanda.

"Detective Gallagher here," a deep voice barked into the phone.

"This is Beth Kent, from the college library," she added, in case he'd forgotten her.

"I remember."

"I'm calling about Amanda."

Brady's voice was decidedly cool as he said, "I'm not sure I'm the person you should be speaking to about her."

"There's been an accident."

His tone immediately changed to one of harsh concern. "Involving Amanda?"

"Not directly." Beth's answer was somewhat disjointed. "Helen, she's one of the assistants in my department. Well, she had a heart attack this afternoon, here in the library."

"I'm very sorry to hear that. I don't know Helen well, but I know Amanda admires her very much."

"Amanda is blaming herself for what happened."

"Blaming herself? Why?"

"Because she'd blown up at Helen a few hours before." Beth then went on to briefly explain the situation, ending with, "I've called every place I can think of, I even drove over to Amanda's house, but there's no sign of her. She's been gone over four hours now, and I'm getting worried."

"You said the emergency room nurse told you that Amanda had been there?"

"Yes, but only for a moment, only long enough to be told that Helen's condition was still critical. Brady, do you have any idea where she could've gone?"

"I might," he replied. "It's a long shot, but it's worth a try. I'll get back to you, Beth. And thanks for calling me. You did the right thing."

It might be egotistical of him to think that Amanda would even remember going to his mountain, but something inside of Brady told him that that's where she was. He had to find her. If she was suffering from the guilt of Helen's heart attack, there was no knowing what her state of mind might be. Hell, he knew firsthand how devastating guilt could be, how destructive.

God, that bluff was high. What if she'd fallen along the path or, worse, gotten too close to the edge and slipped. The possibility alone was enough to send him rushing out into the winter night. He slid behind the wheel of the unmarked squad car, using its siren to hasten his way. At the speed he was traveling, it didn't take long to reach the pulloff he'd shown Amanda.

Her Porsche was there, spotlighted by his car's headlights. Grabbing a flashlight from the dash, he rushed over to her car, but it was empty and unlocked. Brady grimly noted Amanda's purse still sitting on the passenger seat. His cautious Mandy must have been in one hell of a state to leave her purse behind and the car unlocked.

Wasting no more time, he hastened up the path leading to the bluff, calling Amanda's name all the while. There was no response. His heart was in his throat, his thoughts filled with dread. Then he saw her.

She was standing near the edge, her back turned to him, seemingly blind to her surroundings and the possible danger of her proximity to what amounted to a sheer drop.

"I thought I might find you here." Brady spoke calmly, knowing that it might be dangerous to startle her. "Come away from the edge, Mandy."

She slowly shook her head.

"I checked with the hospital," he fibbed, stealthily moving closer all the while. "Helen is going to be all right." This wasn't the time to worry about ethics; he had to get her away from that dangerous precipice.

Amanda slowly turned, taking a few steps toward him.

"Helen's going to be all right," he repeated, desperately hoping it was true. "How about you? Are you all right?"

Amanda again shook her head.

Brady stealthily positioned himself between her and the edge of the bluff before continuing. "It's late, Mandy. Time to come home."

"It was my fault," she whispered in a choked

voice that tore at his heart.

"What was?" he asked, although he already knew what her answer would be.

"Helen's heart attack."

Brady now stood close enough to reach out a hand and stroke her honey-gold hair, but in light of her obviously fragile state he restrained himself, letting his voice do the soothing. "It wasn't your fault."

"Yes, it was. I told her those books had to be shelved today and I made her do all that heavy work."

"Mandy, you had no way of knowing —"

"I should've known," she interrupted fiercely. "I should've noticed how tired she was. There must've been signs and I should've seen them."

"Mandy." He cautiously took her hand, wincing at its iciness. "How long have you been up here?"

"I'm not sure." She stood before him as docile as a child, yet despairing as only an adult can.

"It's time to go home," he told her again.

She numbly shook her head.

"Mandy, listen to me." He reached out to cup her chin with his hand, ensuring her attention. "You're human, just like the rest of us. You're not all-knowing. And while it's natural that you might be feeling guilty right now, this wasn't your fault. You didn't wish this on Helen and you can't keep blaming yourself."

"You don't understand," she cried, trying to escape his hold.

"Don't I?" was his bitter reply. "Don't you

think there are things in my life that I feel guilty about? Things that I would've done differently?"

"But Helen could've died because of me," Amanda sobbed, her voice strangled with guilt.

"She's still living because of you. Beth told me that you administered CPR until the paramedics arrived. That probably saved Helen's life!"

Amanda turned away, refusing to surrender her guilt. Brady's grip shifted to her shoulders, not allowing her to move. "Listen to me, lady. You can't give in to this. I'm not going to let you wallow in guilt."

"How do you know how I feel?" she flared.

Brady's voice was flat as he replied, "Because I know what it's really like to be the cause of someone's death."

Chapter Eleven

His words stilled her attempted flight. "Brady?" His name came out in a twisted croak.

"It's too cold up here to hold a discussion." He held out his hand. "Come back to the car with me, I'll tell you then."

She allowed Brady to guide her down the path to their parked cars and didn't demur when he hustled her into the police department's car. Brady turned the heater up and the two-way radio down. Only then did he begin his story.

"It happened when I was a kid." He paused to take a deep breath. Obviously, even now, this was a difficult matter for him to discuss. "You know that deserted stone quarry outside of town?"

He waited for her nod before continuing. "A group of older kids used to go there to swim and one day I tagged along. There were signs posted warning that swimming was forbidden, but they were ignored. When I got out of my depth and started going down, the other kids panicked."

Caught up as she was in the traumatic chapter from his past, Amanda found her own pain subsiding.

"A guy fishing nearby heard them yelling and came to check out the commotion. He immediately jumped in to save me. Somehow he got me to the shore, but he . . ." Brady's voice roughened with pain. ". . . he didn't make it. You see, he hadn't stopped to take off any of his clothes and they weighed him down."

Amanda felt his suffering. It gripped her throat, blocking her speech. But there was still more to come.

"The man who saved my life at the cost of his own was an off-duty cop. I spent years blaming myself and wallowing in the guilt. I felt there was no direction to my life. I joined the army hoping to find some purpose, but it wasn't the answer."

Brady shifted in his seat, resting one arm on the steering wheel. "My dad was the one who finally brought me out of it. He was the smartest man I ever knew. He didn't have a college degree, but he had more common sense than any scholar. When he discovered he had cancer, he sat me down and told me some things I'll never forget . . ."

Brady's voice trailed off, his thoughts obviously on his deceased father. "He told me that guilt was one of the most devastating of all human emotions, and that I had two choices. I could either let it kill my spirit or I could learn from it and go on. After he died I went to the police academy, then came back to Deerfield. I had found my purpose in life."

"That's why you stayed in Deerfield and joined the police department?" she softly questioned.

Brady nodded. "I felt in some way that I was

repaying the debt I owed to the guy who gave his life for mine. So you see, Mandy," he quietly summed up, "I do know what you're feeling and I know how paralyzing that load of guilt can be."

Amanda could hold back the tears no longer. She sat there, her face buried in her hands, and she cried. Cried for Helen's age, for Brady's youth, and for her future — a future with Brady that she'd given up. Brady winced at her outpouring of emotion, regretting the cause for it, but knowing that this was nature's way of cauterizing the pain. His wide hand came out to softly rest on her down-bent head, directing her tear-blinded figure into his comforting embrace.

Brady waited until her sobs had subsided and her tears had dried before saying, "Come on. I'll take you home."

"What about my car?" Amanda's voice was husky from crying.

"Give me the keys and I'll go lock it."

While she reached into her coat pocket for the keys, Brady leaned forward to turn up the radio and inform headquarters that he'd found Amanda. Before hanging up the microphone, he asked them to relay the message on to Beth.

Amanda felt numb, the flood of tears leaving her drained. "I'm sorry if I caused any trouble," she wearily apologized, handing over her key chain.

Brady secured the Porsche after he picked up her abandoned purse. Amanda mumbled her thanks as he silently placed it on her lap. Sensing her emotional exhaustion, he made no conversational demands during the drive to her house. He accompanied her inside, whereupon he issued the gruff order that she take a hot bath and change into some warm clothing. Amanda made no protest, her expression still dazed as she trailed upstairs.

As soon as she was out of earshot Brady dialed the hospital to check on Helen's condition. He breathed an audible sigh of relief as the nurse informed him that the older woman was indeed in satisfactory condition and out of danger. Unknowingly Brady had told Amanda the truth. Helen was going to be all right! Now he hoped his Mandy would also recover.

Remembering his mother's cure-all, Brady went into the kitchen and returned with a tray just as Amanda was descending the steps.

She looked at his appetizing offering in surprise. "Chicken soup?"

"You had a package of instant mix in the kitchen," Brady explained somewhat defensively. "Go sit in the living room and drink it."

Amanda complied. "Thank you for making this for me."

He watchfully stood over her, his thumbs hooked in the pockets of his jeans in that characteristic stance of his. "I checked with the hospital and Helen's condition is still stable. She's out of the woods."

Amanda's hand trembled so badly at the good news that she slopped a spoonful of soup back into the bowl. "Thank God," she murmured in a relieved voice.

"Keep eating your soup."

"I don't want any more, thank you," she politely declined. Taking her courage in hand, Amanda spoke again. "Brady, if you have the time, I'd like to talk to you."

"I've got time," was his quiet assurance. He sat on the couch, leaning forward so that his elbows rested on his knees.

Taking a deep breath, she launched into speech. "I'd like to explain why I turned down your marriage proposal."

Brady made no comment.

"As you know, my parents got divorced when I was at a very vulnerable age." She faltered, trying to collect her scattered thoughts. "What I'm trying to say is that it wasn't you I was refusing. It was my own emotions. My parents were very much in love when they got married, yet a decade later they ended up detesting each other. My mother has remarried four times — each time she swears that this is the man for her, that she loves him. But it never lasts. Because of my background I've learned to be very cautious of this thing called love, to distrust its effect on my decision-making."

She risked a nervous glance at Brady, trying to gauge his reaction, but his normally expressive face was masked with restraint. "Why did you come after me tonight?" she asked, for until she knew the answer, she couldn't continue.

"Because I cared."

"Cared?" she repeated as though it were a foreign word.

"That's part of loving, caring about someone else's well-being."

It was certainly part of Brady's loving. He'd proved that time and again.

"I'm sorry I never told you I loved you," she regretted.

"I wouldn't have wanted you to lie."

Brady's bitter response made it clear that he still was in the dark about her feelings. "It wouldn't have been a lie," was her quiet assurance. "I do love you."

Hope flared in his dark eyes, lightening his gaze. "You love me?"

The uncertainty in his voice hurt her. "Yes, I love you. I stupidly thought that if I didn't say the words aloud, the feeling would go away."

"You don't want to love me." His statement was flat with disappointment.

"I didn't want to love anyone," she softly corrected him. "I didn't want the pain that loving would bring. Selfishly I only wanted the joy. Instead of which I ended up with nothing but pain; the joy left when you walked out of my life."

"It's been hell on me too," Brady groaned. "Something inside of me didn't want to believe those things I accused you of, but I couldn't come up with any other explanation."

"The difference in our ages has always bothered

me more than the differences in our backgrounds," she felt compelled to confess.

Brady's glance was wryly self-mocking. "With me it was the opposite."

"I should have realized," she berated herself.

"No more guilt trips, Mandy," he gently admonished.

"I assumed that you understood how I felt about marriage. That's why I was so surprised when you proposed. I tried to tell you then that it was marriage, and not you, that I didn't want. But you wouldn't listen."

"Your refusal hit me like a ton of bricks. I thought that when we made love, you were showing me you loved me."

"I was," she confirmed.

"But you didn't want to. You wanted the feeling to go away."

"These past weeks have proved to me they won't go away. And, Brady, I don't want them to. I don't want you to go away. Stay with me. Let me love you."

"Oh, Mandy." He was beside her in an instant, removing the soup bowl from her nervous grip and carefully setting it on the side table. Then he tugged her up into his arms, enfolding her in that special embrace that she thought she'd never feel again. "When I saw you up there on the bluff, standing so close to the edge . . ." he muttered against her temple. "God, you scared the hell out of me. I don't think you'll have to worry about me being younger; it felt like I aged ten years in that one moment."

"I never intended to jump," she quietly assured him.

"Maybe not, but you could easily have slipped. It's certainly icy enough up there."

Amanda tried to get his mind off such dire possibilities by saying, "I spent most of the afternoon driving around. I was probably only up on your mountain for half an hour."

"When Beth phoned me and told me what happened" — he shuddered against her — "I could imagine what you were going through, blaming yourself for Helen's attack."

"Why didn't you tell me about your past sooner?" she leaned away to ask. "It would've helped me understand more."

"Understand why I was only a Deerfield cop, you mean?"

"No, that's not what I mean. I always knew that you had the capability to be anything you wanted, to do anything, go anywhere. And I will admit to being confused. Confused," she reiterated. "Not disappointed."

Brady pulled her close again. "Would it have made it easier on you if I'd been an accountant?" His words may have been muffled, but her sensitive ears picked up the need for reassurance.

Amanda gave it without hesitation. "No, it wouldn't have made it easier. Besides, if you'd been an accountant I would never have been able to frisk you!"

His chuckle gave her a warm sense of accomplishment and the courage to say, "You're a lover who happens to be a cop, not the other way around."

"After the trauma you've been through today, I think you might need a friend more than a lover tonight." His eyes regarded her with tender concern.

"Don't you want to stay?" she whispered.

"Of course I want to stay," Brady growled. "If I don't kiss you soon, I think I'll go crazy!" His voice regained its serious note as he continued. "But I don't want to make love to you again until you're sure. I can wait."

"I am sure and I can't wait." Her words were a soft invocation to stay. "Life's too short for waiting. Helen's attack made me realize that."

Still Brady held back, cautiously questioning, "Are you sure that what you're experiencing isn't a natural fear of mortality?"

"No, this isn't fear. It's rejoicing. I want to rejoice in you."

The shining certainty of her voice left him in no doubt. "And I want to rejoice in you," was his husky reply.

No more words were spoken until they were upstairs, secluded in the peaceful surroundings of Amanda's bedroom. With the closing of the door came the lowering of their last defenses. They reached out for each other with fervent desperation. So strong was their need that it couldn't be expressed with words; it could only be conveyed through a tight embrace.

In an attempt to ease the intense emotional build-up, Brady shakenly questioned, "What do you call this thing you're wearing?"

"A hostess gown," she mumbled into his shoulder.

"It looks good on you. But I think it would look even better off of you!"

Amanda had no time to ponder on how much she'd missed hearing that teasing inflection in his voice, for Brady had undone her gown's only means of support and it accommodatingly slid to the floor. Her newly bathed skin glowed in the muted light cast by her single bedside lamp. Brady touched her with his eyes, the visual radiance of his gaze igniting whirlwinds of fire that danced across her bare skin.

His arms gathered her in, the softness of her breasts evocatively brushing against the worn cotton of his shirt. His denim-clad thighs were dynamically firm, his elevated desire unmistakable. Amanda leaned into him, her body wantonly adjusting itself to his taut masculine contours. His riffling fingers left their warm imprint in her hair as he wove them through it, his thumb seductively soothing the pulse beating at her temples.

When his head lowered for a kiss, Amanda was more than ready to meet him halfway. The kiss was a union of lips — blending, shaping, touching, tasting, the hunger all-consuming. The coiled intimacy of their tongues was a promising foretaste of things to come.

She felt no embarrassment at the fact that she

was nude while Brady was still fully dressed. Opening her eyes, she gazed at his face. It was etched with emotion, his eyes burning with a raging desire.

Moments later an equally unencumbered Brady took her to bed. They slipped under the damask-covered comforter, the air suddenly chilly on their bare skin. They quickly built up a hollow of warmth. Unlike the last time they'd made love, there was no extended prelude. Their emotions ran too high and too deep for that. Instead there was a concentrated dedication that bordered on reverence.

Like the hands of a master sculptor bringing his creation to life, Brady's adoring fingers stroked every inch of her, leaving Amanda with an undeniable need to have them rest on the one spot that was aching with desire. She soon thought that she could bear the tension no longer and her body twisted against his in search of some kind of satisfaction. Successive, erotically intimate caresses were accompanied by increasing rushes of excitement until the need for fulfillment overcame the sweet anticipation. Her body moved in unison with his until that building tension exploded into recurrent waves of pulsating rhythm. Reality was suspended by an immeasurable exultation as Amanda was propelled into a realm of unsurpassed pleasure.

It wasn't the physical satisfaction alone that brought tears of joy to her eyes. It was the intimacy — the feeling of being close, of being needed, of being loved, of being alive, that she'd craved. Brady's soft kiss to the tip of her nose gave the final passages of their merging an unutterable tenderness, the likes of which she'd never experienced before.

Several hours later Amanda awoke from an almost drugged sleep to the feel of feather-light kisses drifting across the gentle slope of her shoulder. She was curled up on her side, a radiant heat warming her back. That energy source was Brady. Lingering in the dream world between waking and sleeping, the events of last night were savored. Her shoulder rose, seemingly of its own accord, as if her flesh were already fully awake to the pleasure his caress was supplying and wanted more.

Brady was certainly willing to oblige. The same captivating kisses were bestowed along her neck, his fingers threading through the honeyed cloud of her hair to lift it out of his way. When the lobe of her ear was pillaged with nibbling bites, Amanda turned onto her back, offering him her parted lips. Brady groaned and gathered her close for another pilgrimage to love's incandescent altar.

The next time Amanda opened her eyes it was to find Brady still sleeping. She carefully levered herself onto an elbow to study his peaceful features. She loved watching him, noting every quirk until she'd collected what amounted to a running catalog.

Amanda began mentally listing the things she loved about Brady. Odd things came to mind, like the way his hair tumbled over his collar, when he was wearing one! She loved his smile and the way the laugh lines at the corners of his mouth matched those at the corners of his eyes. She loved him on the rare occasions when he was embarrassed, tugging on his hair or scratching one ear. She loved the infinite range of his voice, the way he made the order "come here" sound like a wishful "comemirror." She loved the expressiveness of his looks, the way his eyes widened with boyish humor or teasing kindness.

Then, under a separate heading, was the way he made love: the emotional variety of his kisses, the integral sensitivity of his touch, the caressive finesse of their physical merging. But Brady wasn't just sexy, he was also "snuggable," a man who could inspire both excitement and contentment. A man she would love to spend the rest of her life with!

Amanda kept her plans to herself until after breakfast. Brady had phoned the hospital again to check on Helen's condition, which was improving, and had now joined Amanda at the food-laden kitchen table. He devoured the meal with unconcealed relish, helping himself to seconds.

"Would you pass the toast?" he requested, sliding another rasher of bacon and scrambled eggs onto his plate.

Amanda handed it to him, watching him butter a slice. "Would you marry me?"

Brady slowly lifted his head, certain he must

have misunderstood her. "What did you say?" he asked in a hushed voice.

Observing his shaken expression, she repeated, "Would you marry me?"

Brady looked absolutely overcome, which didn't improve her nerves any! "What changed your mind about marriage?" he finally asked.

"You did. Your love did. I want to spend the rest of my life with you and it seems ridiculous to be afraid of a piece of paper."

"Is that all marriage is to you, a piece of paper?"

"Brady, if I didn't take marriage seriously, I wouldn't have been afraid of it all these years."

He granted her that point. "You're not afraid anymore?"

"I'm afraid you're never going to answer my question," she burst out in anxious exasperation.

She was too nervous to note the telltale gleam in his eyes. "I don't know," he debated. "Do you think we have enough in common? You're well-educated, with a string of degrees, while I'm —"

"One of the most intelligent men I know," she interrupted him. "And we do have a lot in common . . . unless you lied when you said you loved me?"

His grin gave him away. "You know better than that."

"You argued with me deliberately, didn't you." It was an accusation, not a question.

"I just wanted to make sure you knew what you were getting into."

"Oh, I know, all right," she assured him, her slanting look promising retribution. "I may not have before, but I do now."

"In that case the answer's yes!" Brady stood to tug her out of her chair. In a melodramatic gesture reminiscent of *Gone With the Wind*, he swept her off her feet and into his arms. Amanda was carried out of the kitchen and through the hall, but halfway up the stairway Brady paused, pivoting to plonk down on the sixth step.

"What's wrong?" she asked from her vantage point atop his knees.

"Rest stop," he gasped in an exaggerated manner.

"Rhett Butler didn't have to rest, and he carried Scarlet up a flight of stairs twice this high."

"Ah, but he hadn't just eaten a huge breakfast and then been proposed to!"

"That's why I ordered a younger model," Amanda impishly replied. Perched as she was on Brady's lap, she was several inches taller than he and it gave her a rush of power. But her regal sovereignty dissolved when he deliberately blew in her ear, setting her off in a fit of giggles.

"I don't think the stairs are a suitable site for a seduction scene," she chortled.

He laughed at her abundance of *s*'s. "Is that supposed to be a tongue twister?"

"Last one in bed has to do the breakfast dishes," Amanda shrieked, leaping off his lap and up the stairs before Brady could make a move to stop her.

Not that he wanted to. He had the same destination in mind himself!

"I think it's a tie," she gasped as they simultaneously collapsed on the bed. "What do you think?"

Brady's attention was distracted by her heaving breasts, their rapid rise and fall inciting his passion. "I think we should get in some more practice before our honeymoon," was his husky suggestion. "To make sure we get it right."

"And left."

"Oh, I'll cover all the angles," he assured her, removing her robe.

"I never doubted it for a minute." The dusky tips of her breasts impudently teased his bare chest. Her hands, intimately resting on his hips, registered his involuntary shudder at the heated magic of her touch. Amanda smiled mischievously. "Where would you like to go for our honeymoon?"

"To bed!" Brady growled, devouring her with gusto.

Amanda teasingly held him at bay. "Where?"

"How about the Alps?" he delighted her by suggesting. "I could show you Garmisch."

Undoing the snap on his jeans, she purred, "You could show me a lot of things, Detective Gallagher!"

He spent the rest of the day doing just that!